RUNAWAY TEMPTATION

MAUREEN CHILD

MILLS & BOON

First Published in Great Britain 2018
by Mills & Boon, an imprint of HarperCollins*Publishers*
1 London Bridge Street, London, SE1 9GF

© 2018 Harlequin Books S.A.

Special thanks and acknowledgement are given to Maureen Child
for her contribution to the Texas Cattleman's Club:
Bachelor Auction miniseries.

AW ISBN: 978-0-263-07691-2

MIX
Paper from
responsible sources
FSC **FSC C007454**
www.fsc.org

This book is produced from independently certified FSC™ paper
to ensure responsible forest management.
For more information visit www.harpercollins.co.uk/green.

Printed and bound in Great Britain
by CPI Group (UK) Ltd, Croydon, CR0 4YY

Maureen Child writes for the Mills & Boon Desire line and can't imagine a better job. A seven-time finalist for a prestigious Romance Writers of America RITA® Award, Maureen is an author of more than one hundred romance novels. Her books regularly appear on bestseller lists and have won several awards, including a Prism Award, a National Readers' Choice Award, a Colorado Romance Writers Award of Excellence and a Golden Quill Award. She is a native Californian but has recently moved to the mountains of Utah.

To Carter and Cade. For the hugs. For the laughs.
For the love. For the future.

One

"I hate weddings." Caleb Mackenzie ran his index finger around the inside of his collar. But that didn't do a thing to loosen the tie he wore, or to rid himself of the "wish I were anywhere but here" thoughts racing through his mind. "I feel like I'm overdressed for my own hanging."

Caleb wasn't real fond of suits. Sure, he had a wide selection of them since he needed them for meetings and business deals. But he was much more comfortable in jeans, a work shirt and his favorite boots, running his ranch, the Double M. Still, as the ranch grew, he found himself in the dreaded suits more and more often because expansion called for meeting bankers and investors on their turf.

Right now, though, he'd give plenty to be on a horse riding out across the open range. Caleb knew his ranch hands were getting the work done, but there were stock ponds to check on, a pregnant mare he was keeping an eye on and a hay field still to harvest and store.

Yet instead, here he stood, in the hot Texas sun, in an elegant suit and shining black boots. He tugged the brim of his gray Stetson down lower over his eyes and slanted a look at the mob of people slowly streaming into the Texas Cattleman's Club for the ceremony and reception.

If he could, he'd slip out of town. But it was too late now.

"You're preaching to the choir, man."

Caleb nodded at his friend Nathan Battle. If he had to be there, at least he had company.

Nathan settled his cowboy hat more firmly on his head and sent a frown toward his pretty, very pregnant wife standing with a group of her friends. "I swear, I think Amanda really enjoys it when I have to wear a suit."

"Women'll kill you." Caleb sighed and leaned back against his truck. As hot as he was, he was in no hurry to go inside and take a seat for the ceremony. Given a choice, he'd always choose to be outside under the sky. Even a hot and humid August day was preferable to being trapped inside.

"Maybe, but it's not a bad way to go—" Nathan broke off and asked, "Why're you here, anyway? Not like you've got a wife to make you do what you don't want to do." As soon as the words left his mouth, Nathan winced and said, "Sorry, man. Wasn't thinking."

"No problem." Caleb gritted his teeth and swallowed the knot of humiliation that could still rise up and choke him from time to time. The thing about small towns was, not only did everyone know what everybody else was doing—nobody ever forgot a damn thing. Four years since the day his wedding hadn't happened and everyone in Royal remembered.

But then, it wasn't like he'd forgotten, either.

Amazing, really. In the last few years, this town had seen tornadoes, killer storms, blackmailers and even a man coming back from the dead. But somehow, the memory of Caleb's botched wedding day hadn't been lost in the tidal wave of events.

Nathan shifted position, his discomfort apparent. Caleb couldn't help him with that. Hell, he was uncomfortable, too. But to dispel the tension, Caleb said lightly, "You should have worn your uniform."

As town sheriff, Nathan was rarely dressed in civilian clothes. The man was most comfortable in his khaki uniform, complete with badge, walking the town, talking to everyone and keeping an eye on things. He snorted. "Yeah, that wouldn't fly with Amanda."

A soft smile curved his friend's mouth and just for a second or two, Caleb envied the other man. "When's the new baby due again?"

"Next month."

And, though he knew the answer already, Caleb asked, "How many will that make now?"

Nathan grinned and shot him a wink. "This one makes four."

A set of four-year-old twin boys, a two-year-old girl and now another one. "How many are you planning, anyway?"

Nathan shrugged. "Who says there's a plan? Mandy loves babies, and I have to say I do enjoy making them."

Marriage. Family. All of that slipped by him four

years ago. And now that Nathan had reminded him, Caleb idly wondered how many kids he and Meg might have had by now if things had gone the way he'd expected. But the night before their wedding, Meg had run off with Caleb's brother, Mitch. Now the two of them lived on the family ranch with their set of twins. Three years old, the boy and girl ran wild around the ranch and Caleb put whatever he might have felt for kids of his own into those two.

There might still be tension between him and his brother, Mitch, not to mention Meg. But he loved those kids more than he would have thought possible.

"Mitch and Meg still out of town?" Nathan asked, glancing around as if half expecting to see them walking up.

"Yeah. Visiting Meg's family." And Caleb had been enjoying the respite.

"That's one way to get out of going to a summer wedding."

"Amen." Caleb loosened his tie a little. Felt like he was beginning to melt out here in the sun. He spared a glance at the sky and watched a few lazy white clouds drifting along. "Who plans a wedding in August, anyway? Hotter than the halls of hell out here."

"You know how the Goodmans are," Nathan answered. "The old man figures he knows everything and the rest of them—except Brooke—just fall in line. Probably his idea to hold it in high summer. No doubt he was aiming for it to be the talk of the town."

That sounded like Simon Goodman. Though the man was Caleb's lawyer, that was more from inertia than anything else. Goodman had been Caleb's father's lawyer and when the elder Mackenzie died, Caleb just never bothered to change the situation. So his own in-action had brought him here. Truth be told, Caleb usually avoided attending *any* weddings since it inevitably brought up old memories that he'd just as soon bury.

"Anyway," Nathan said, pushing past the uncomfortable pause in the conversation, "I'm the town sheriff. I'm sort of *forced* to be at these society things. Why the hell did you come?"

Caleb snorted. "Normally, I wouldn't have. But Simon Goodman's still the ranch attorney. So it's business to be at his son Jared's wedding." And he made a mental note to do something about that real soon. He shrugged. "If Mitch and Meg had been in town I'd have forced my brother to go instead of me. But since they're gone, I'm stuck."

Served him right, Caleb told himself, for letting things slide. He never should have kept Simon on. He and Caleb's father had been great friends so that didn't speak well of the man.

He'd let the lawyer relationship stand mainly because it was easier than taking time away from work to find someone new. Between running the ranch and ex-panding the oil-rich field discovered only twenty years before, Caleb had been too damn busy to worry about a lawyer he only had to deal with a few times a year.

Looking for a change of subject, Caleb said, "Since you're here, that means the new deputy's in charge, right?"

Nathan winced. "Yeah. Jeff's doing fine."

Caleb laughed. "Sure, I can hear the confidence in your voice."

Sighing, Nathan pushed one hand through his hair and shook his head. "With Jack retired, I needed a deputy and Jeff Baker's working out. But he's from Houston so it's taking him some time to get used to small town living."

Caleb had heard about it. Jeff was about thirty and a little too strict on the law and order thing for Royal. The new deputy had handed out more speeding tickets in the last six months than Nathan had in years. Folks in Royal hit an empty road and they just naturally picked up speed. Jeff Baker wasn't making many friends.

"Hell," Caleb said, "I've lived here my whole life and I'm still not used to it."

"I hear that," Nathan replied, shifting his gaze to where his wife stood with a group of friends. "But I've been getting a lot of complaints about the tickets Jeff's handing out."

Caleb laughed. "He's not going to slow anybody down."

"Maybe not," Nathan agreed with a nod. "But he's going to keep trying."

"I expect so," Caleb mused, then glanced over at Nathan's wife who was smiling and waving one hand. "I think Amanda wants you."

Straightening up, Nathan gave a heartfelt sigh. "That's it, then. I'll see you after. At the reception?"

"I don't think so. Soon as I'm clear, I'm headed back to the ranch."

Another sigh. "Lucky bastard."

Caleb grinned and watched his friend head toward the Texas Cattleman's Club building. The place was a one-story, rambling sort, made of dark wood and stone, boasting a tall slate roof. It was a part of Royal and had been for generations. Celebrations of all kinds had been held there and today, it was a wedding. One he'd have to attend in just a few minutes.

Shelby Arthur stared at her own reflection and hardly recognized herself. She supposed all brides felt like that on their wedding day, but for her, the effect was terrifying.

Her long, dark auburn curls were pulled back from her face to hang down to the center of her back. Her veil poofed out around her head and her green eyes narrowed at the gown she hated. A ridiculous number of yards of white tulle made Shelby look like a giant marshmallow caught in netting. The dress was her about-to-be-mother-in-law's doing. She'd insisted that the Goodmans had a reputation to maintain in Royal and the simple off-the-shoulder gown Shelby had chosen wouldn't do the trick.

So instead, she was looking at a stranger wearing an old-fashioned gown with long, lacy sleeves, a cinched waist and full skirt, and a neckline that was so high she felt as if she were choking.

"Thank God for air-conditioning," she muttered, otherwise in the sweltering Texas heat, she'd be little more than a tulle-covered puddle on the floor. She half turned to get a look at the back of the dress and finally sighed. She looked like one of those crocheted dolls her grandmother used to make to cover up spare toilet paper rolls.

Shelby was about to get married in a dress she hated, a veil she didn't want, to a man she wasn't sure she *liked*, much less loved. How did she get to this point?

"Oh, God. What am I doing?" The whisper was strained but heartfelt.

She'd left her home in Chicago to marry Jared Goodman. But now that he was home in Texas, under his awful father's thumb, Jared was someone she didn't even know. Her whirlwind romance had morphed into a nightmare and now she was trapped.

She took a breath, blew it out and asked her reflection, "What are you doing?"

"Good question."

Shelby jumped, startled by the sudden appearance of Jared's mother. The woman was there, behind her in the mirror, bustling into the room. Margaret Goodman was tall and painfully thin. Her face was all sharp angles and her blue eyes were small and judgmental. Her graying blond hair was scraped back from her face into a bun that incongruously sported a circlet of yellow rosebuds. The beige suit she wore was elegant if boring and was so close to the color of her hair and skin the woman simply disappeared into her clothes.

If only, Shelby thought.

"Your veil should be down over your face," Margaret chastised, hurrying over to do just that.

As the veil fell across her vision, Shelby had a momentary panic attack and felt as though she couldn't breathe through that all-encompassing tulle curtain, so she whipped it back again. Taking a deep breath, she said, "I'm sorry, I can't—"

"You will." Margaret stepped back, took a look, then moved to tug at the skirt of the wedding gown. "We're going for a very traditional, chaste look here. It's unseemly that this wedding is happening so quickly. The town will be gossiping for months, watching for a swollen belly."

Shelby sucked in a gulp of air. "I've told you already, I'm not pregnant."

"We'll soon see, won't we?" One blond eyebrow lifted over pale blue eyes. "The Goodman family has a reputation in this town and I expect you to do nothing to besmirch it."

"Besmirch?" Who even talked like that, Shelby thought wildly. It was as if she'd dropped into a completely different universe. Suddenly, she missed Chicago—her friends, her *life*, so much she ached with it.

Moving to Texas with a handsome, well-connected cowboy who had swept her off her feet had seemed like an adventure at the time. Now she was caught up in a web that seemed inescapable. Her fiancé was a stranger, his mother a blatant enemy and his brother had a way of looking at Shelby that had her wishing she'd paid more attention in self-defense class.

Jared's father, Simon, was no better, making innuendoes that he probably thought were clever but gave Shelby the outright creeps. The only bright spot in the Goodman family was Jared's sister, Brooke, and she couldn't help Shelby with what was about to happen.

Somehow, she had completely lost control of her own life and now she stood there in a mountain of tulle trying to find enough scraps of who she was to cling to.

"Once the ceremony is finished, we'll all go straightaway to the reception," Margaret was saying.

Oh, God.

"You and Jared will, of course, be in the receiving line until every guest has been welcomed personally. The photographer can then indulge in the necessary photos for precisely fifteen minutes, after which you and Jared will reenter the reception for the ceremonial first toast." Margaret paused long enough to glance into the mirror herself and smooth hair that wouldn't dare fall out of place. "Mr. Goodman is an important man and as his family *we* will do all we can to support him. Is that understood?" Her gaze, hard and cold, shot to Shelby's. "When you've returned from your honeymoon…"

Her stomach sank even further. She wouldn't have been surprised to see it simply drop out of her body and fall *splat* onto the floor. Her day was scheduled. Her honeymoon was scheduled and she had no doubt at all that her *life* would be carefully laid out for her, complete with bullet points.

How had it all come to this?

For their honeymoon, Shelby had wanted to see Paris. Instead, Jared's mother had insisted they go to Philadelphia so Shelby could be introduced to the eastern branch of the Goodman family. And much to her dismay, Jared was simply doing as he was told with no regard at all for Shelby. He'd changed so much since coming back to Texas that she hardly recognized the man anymore.

Margaret was still talking. Fixing a steely gaze on the mirror, she met Shelby's eyes. "When you return to Texas, you will of course give up your ridiculous business and be the kind of wife to Jared that will enable him to further his own law career."

"Oh, I don't think—"

"You'll be a Goodman," Margaret snapped, brooking no argument.

Shelby swallowed hard. When they'd met in Chicago, Jared had talked about his ranch in Texas. He'd let her believe that he was a cowboy who happened to also have a law degree. And yes, she could admit that the fantasy of being with a cowboy had really appealed to her. But mostly, he'd talked about their having a family and that had sealed the deal for Shelby.

She'd told herself then that she could move her professional organizer business anywhere. But from the moment Jared had introduced her to his family, Margaret had made it clear that her "little business" was hardly appropriate.

Shelby met her own eyes in the mirror and read the desperation there. Maybe all of this would be easier to take if she was madly in love with Jared. But the truth was, she'd fooled herself from the beginning. This wasn't love. It couldn't be. The romance, the excitement, had all worn off, like the luster of sterling silver as soon as it was tarnished. Rather than standing up for himself, Jared was completely cowed by his family and that really didn't bode well for Shelby's future.

Margaret checked the slim gold watch on her wrist, clucked her tongue and headed for the door. "The music will begin in exactly five minutes." She stopped, glanced over her shoulder and added, "My husband will be here to escort you down the aisle since you don't have a father of your own."

Shelby's mouth dropped open as the other woman left the room. Stunned, she realized Margaret had tossed that last bit with venom, as if Shelby had arranged for her father to die ten years ago just so he could disrupt Margaret Goodman's wedding scenario.

She shivered at the thought of Simon Goodman. She didn't want him anywhere near her, let alone escorting her, touching her. And even worse, she was about to promise to be in Simon's family for the rest of her life.

"Nope, can't do it." She glanced at her own reflection and in a burst of fury ripped her veil off her face.

Then, blowing a stray auburn lock from her forehead, she gathered up the skirt of the voluminous gown in both arms.

"Have to hurry," she muttered, giving herself the impetus she needed to make a break for it before it was too late. If she didn't leave now, she'd be *married* into the most awful family she'd ever known.

"Not going to happen," she reassured herself as she tentatively opened the door and peered out.

Thankfully, there was no one in this section of the TCC. They were all in the main room, waiting for the ceremony to start. In the distance, she heard the soft thrum of harp music playing as an underscore to the rise and fall of conversations. She could only guess what they'd all be talking about soon.

That wasn't her problem, though. Clutching her wedding gown high enough to keep it out of her way, she hurried down the hall and toward the nearest exit.

She thought she heard someone calling her name, but Shelby didn't let that stop her. She hit the front door and started running. It was blind panic that kept her moving. After all, she had nowhere to go. She didn't know hardly anyone in Royal besides the Goodman family. But she kept moving because the unknown was wildly better than the alternative.

Her veil caught on one of the porch posts and yanked her back briefly. But Shelby ripped the stupid thing off her head, tiara and all, and tossed it to the ground. Then she was off again, tearing around a corner and running smack into a brick wall.

Well, that's what it felt like.

A tall, gorgeous brick wall who grabbed her upper arms to steady her, then smiled down at her with humor in his eyes. He had enough sex appeal to light up the city of Houston and the heat from his hands, sliding down her body, made everything inside her jolt into life.

"Aren't you headed the wrong way?" he asked, and the soft drawl in his deep voice awakened a single thought in her mind.

Oh, boy.

Two

A *real* cowboy.

Shelby tipped her head back to look up at him and caught the flash of surprise in his gaze as he reached out to steady her. Ridiculously enough, considering the situation—running away from her own wedding—she felt a hot blast of something...*amazing.*

The cowboy had shaggy light brown hair, icy-blue eyes, a strong jaw and a gray cowboy hat tipped down low on his forehead. He wore a black suit, crisp white shirt with a dove-gray tie and oh, sweet mama Lou, shining black cowboy boots. His hands were strong and warm on her upper arms and a slow smile curved his mouth as he took in what she was wearing.

And the soft drawl in his deep voice really worked for her. He was everything Jared wasn't. Although, even as she thought it, Shelby reminded herself that her judgment had been so crappy about Jared that she could be just as wrong about Mr. Tall, Dark and Yummy.

"Hey now," he said, that deep voice rolling along her spine again. "Are you all right?"

"Absolutely not," she said firmly. The humor in his eyes was gone, replaced by concern and she responded to it. "I have to get out of here. Now. Can you help me?"

His eyes narrowed on her and his delectable mouth moved into a grim slash. "You're running out on your wedding?"

Disapproval practically radiated from him and Shelby's spine went stiff as a board in reaction. "Just as fast as I can," she said. "Can you help me?"

Before he could say yes or no, another voice erupted behind her.

"Shelby! What the devil do you think you're doing?"

Spinning around until the cowboy was at her back, Shelby watched as Margaret Goodman stalked toward her, fire in her eyes. "Your guests are waiting."

"They're not my guests," Shelby said. Heck, the only people she knew in Royal was the family she was supposed to marry into and frankly, if they were the best this town had to offer, she was ready to *run* back to Chicago.

"Of course they are." Margaret waved her hand impatiently, dismissing Shelby's argument. "Don't be foolish."

Shelby moved back until she felt the cowboy's tall, strong body press up against hers. Cowardly? Maybe, but she'd live with it. Right now, this tall, exceptionally well-built man was the safest spot she could find.

Margaret's gaze snapped to the cowboy. "Caleb, bring her along inside right this minute."

Caleb. His name was Caleb. For a second, Shelby worried that he might do just that. After all, he didn't know her and the Goodman family, as they kept telling her, were a big deal here in Royal. Maybe he wasn't the safe harbor she'd thought he was.

Then the cowboy stepped out from behind her and moved to partially block Shelby from the woman glaring at her. While Shelby watched, he tipped his hat and said, "I don't take orders from you, Mrs. Goodman."

Margaret inhaled through her nose and if she could have set the cowboy on fire, she clearly would have. "Fine. *Please* bring her along inside. The wedding is about to start."

"Well now," Caleb said slowly, that deep drawl caressing every word, "I don't believe the lady wants to go back inside."

"No," Shelby said, exhaling in a rush. "I do not."

"There you go. She sounds pretty sure," Caleb said, shrugging as if he couldn't have cared less which way this confrontation turned out.

"Well, I'm sure, too." Margaret took a menacing step forward. "This woman is engaged to my son, God help me."

Insulted, Shelby frowned, but the older woman kept going.

"We have a club full of people waiting for the ceremony to begin and the Goodman family has a reputation to uphold in Royal. I refuse to allow some city tramp to ruin it."

"Tramp?" Okay, now she was more sure than ever that running had been the right thing to do. The very idea of having to deal with this woman as a *relative* for the rest of her life gave her cold chills.

Shelby took a step toward the woman with the plan to tell Margaret exactly what she thought of her. But the cowboy alongside her grabbed her arm to hold her in place.

"That's enough, Margaret," he said quietly.

"It's not nearly enough." Margaret fired a hard look at the cowboy before shifting her gaze back to Shelby. "You stay out of this, Caleb Mackenzie. This has nothing to do with you."

Though the urge to stand here and have it out with this appalling woman was so strong Shelby was almost quivering, she knew it would be a waste of time. And, since the most important thing was to escape before any more Goodmans showed up, she turned her head to stare up at the man beside her.

"Can you get me out of here?" Shelby asked, staring up into those cool, blue eyes.

"What?" Ignoring Margaret, the man looked at her as if he hadn't heard her right.

"Take me somewhere," she blurted, and didn't even think about the fact that she didn't know this man. Right now it was enough that Margaret clearly couldn't stand him. The enemy of my enemy, and all that.

"You want me to help you run out on the man waiting for you at the altar?"

"Well, when you put it like that, it sounds terrible," Shelby admitted, shifting uneasily from foot to foot.

"What other way is there to put it?"

"Okay fine. I'm a terrible human being," she whispered frantically as Margaret heaped curses on her head. "And I'll apologize to Jared later. But right now…"

Caleb stared down at her as if trying to see inside her. And Shelby was grateful that he couldn't. Because right now, her insides were tangled up into so many knots she'd probably look like a crazy person. Heck, she *felt* like a crazy person. One that had just made a break from the asylum and was now looking for a ride back to sanity.

Hitching the yards of tulle higher in her arms, Shelby murmured, "Margaret said your name's Caleb, right?"

"That's right."

God, his voice was so deep it seemed to echo out around her. His blue eyes were focused on her and Shelby felt a flutter of something she'd never felt for the man she'd almost married. Probably not a good thing. "Look, I don't have much time. If you can't help me, I need to find someone else. Fast." She took a breath and blew it out again. "So. Are you going to help me, Caleb?"

One corner of his mouth lifted briefly. "What's your name?"

"Shelby," she said, mesmerized by the motion of that mouth. "Shelby Arthur."

"I'm Caleb Mackenzie," he said. "My truck's over there."

He jerked his head toward a big, top-of-the-line black pickup that shone like midnight, its chrome bumpers glittering in the sun. At that moment, the huge black truck looked like a magical carriage there to transport her away from a nightmare. Shelby sighed in relief and practically sprinted for it.

"Where are you going?" Margaret's voice, loud, desperate, followed her. "You can't leave! What will people think?"

"Whatever the hell they want to," Caleb tossed over his shoulder. "Just like always."

He opened the passenger door and helped Shelby to

climb in. "We have to hurry," she said, throwing frantic looks at the building behind them.

"It'd be easier if you didn't have so damn much dress," he muttered, grabbing a fistful of the material and stuffing it into the truck.

"Never mind the dress," she said, staring down at him. She was doing it. Getting away. But she wasn't gone yet. Grabbing at the dress, she shoved it between her knees and then ignored the rest of the hot mess gown still hanging down the side of the truck. "Just get in and *drive*."

He looked up at her and again, Shelby felt that rush of something hot and unexpected. That was just too weird. A few minutes ago, she'd been set to marry another man and now she was getting all warm and shivery for a cowboy in shining armor? What was *wrong* with her?

"Yes, ma'am," he said. "You're the boss." Then he slammed the truck door, leaving a couple of feet of dress hanging out beneath the bottom.

Shelby didn't care. All she wanted was to get away. To feel free. She pushed her hair out of her face as it slipped from the intricate knots it had been wound into. While Caleb walked around the front of the truck, she stared out the window at the woman still cursing her. Shelby had the oddest desire to wave goodbye and smile. But she didn't. Instead, she looked away from her would-be mother-in-law and when Caleb climbed into the truck and fired it up, she took her first easy breath. When he threw it into gear and drove from the parking lot, Shelby laughed at the wild release pumping through her.

He glanced at her. "Are you crazy?"

She shook her head and grinned. "Not anymore. I think I'm cured."

* * *

Caleb told himself that if she wasn't crazy herself, she was probably a carrier. How else did he explain why he was driving down the long, nearly empty road toward his ranch with a runaway bride sitting beside him?

Two words repeated in his brain. *Runaway bride.* Hell, he was helping do to Jared what Mitch and Meg had done to *him* four years ago. Was this some kind of backward Karma?

Caleb shot a sideways look at his passenger. The dress was god-awful, but it was fitted to her body like a damn glove. Her high, full breasts were outlined behind yet another layer of lace. The high neck only made a man wonder what was being hidden. Long sleeves caressed her arms and a damn mountain of white net poofed out around her body even while she fought it down.

Her face was pale, making the handful of freckles across her nose stand out like firelight in a snowstorm. While he watched, she rolled down the window and her hair was suddenly a wild tangle of dark red curls flying in the wind.

She closed her eyes, smiled into the wind, then turned to look at him and smiled even wider. "Thanks for the rescue."

Yeah. He'd rescued her and helped to humiliate Jared, just as he himself had once been. Caleb didn't much care for Jared Goodman, but that didn't make what he'd done any easier to take.

"Why'd you wait to run?" he asked.

"What?"

"Why wait until the last damn minute to change your mind?"

"Good question." She sighed, pushed her hair back, then propped her elbow on the door. "I kept thinking it would get better, I guess. Instead, it just got worse."

He could understand that. It was the Goodmans, after all.

"And you couldn't leave before today?"

She looked at him and frowned. "I could have. But I gave my word. I said I'd marry Jared—"

"But you didn't."

"Couldn't," she corrected, shaking her head. "Staring at myself in the mirror, wearing this hideous dress, listening to Margaret tell me about the honeymoon plans *she* made…" Her voice died off and it was a few seconds before she spoke again. "It finally hit me that I just couldn't go through with it. So I ran. I suppose you think that's cowardly."

"Well…"

She shifted in her seat, hiking all of that white fabric higher until it was above her knees, displaying a pair of long, tanned legs. When she stopped just past her knees, Caleb was more than a little disappointed.

He looked back at the road. Way safer than looking at her.

"You're wrong," she said. "It took more strength to run than it would have to stay."

Frowning to himself, Caleb thought about that for a minute. Was it possible she had a point?

She threw both hands up, the fabric spilled off her lap to the floor and she muttered a curse as she gathered it all up again to hold on her lap. Caleb spared another quick look at her long, tanned legs, then told himself to keep his eyes on the road.

"Honestly," she said, "I could have gone through with

it and not been called a 'tramp.' I could have stayed, knowing that I didn't really love Jared after all, but going through with the wedding to avoid the embarrassment. But it wasn't right for me or fair to Jared for me to marry him knowing I didn't want to be married, especially to him, you know what I mean?"

Before he could say anything, she rolled right on.

Waving one hand, then grabbing up fabric again with another curse, she said, "I know he'll be angry and probably hurt today but sooner or later, he's going to see that I did the right thing and who knows, maybe he'll even *thank* me for it at some point."

"Don't hold your breath," Caleb muttered.

"What? Never mind." Shaking her head, she took a deep breath, looked out over the open road and said, "Even if he doesn't thank me out loud, he'll be glad. Eventually. This is better. I mean, I don't know what to do *now*, but this is definitely better. For both of us."

"You sound sure."

She looked at him again until he felt compelled to meet those forest green eyes of hers however briefly. "I am," she said. "So thank you. Again."

"You're welcome." Caleb didn't know what the hell he was supposed to do with her, so he was headed home. Back at the ranch, she could call her own family. Or a cab. And then she could be on her way and he could get out of this damn suit.

With that thought firmly in mind, Caleb focused on the familiar road stretching out ahead of him and did his best to ignore the beautiful woman sitting way too close to him.

There were wide sweeps of open land dotted with the scrub oaks that grew like weeds in East Texas. Here and there were homes and barns, with horses in paddocks and cattle grazing in the fields. The sky was the kind of clear, deep blue he'd only ever seen in Texas and those few gusting clouds he'd glimpsed earlier had gathered up a few friends.

Everything was absolutely normal. Except for the bride in his truck.

"Weird day," he muttered.

"It is, isn't it?" She whipped her hair out of her eyes to look at him. "I never thought I'd be a fugitive from my own wedding. And I know I've said this already, but thank you. I kind of threw myself at you and didn't give you much room to back off, so I really appreciate you riding to the rescue."

"I could have said no," he reminded her.

She tilted her head to one side and studied him. "No, I don't think you could have."

He snorted. "Is that right?"

"Yeah. I think so." She shook her head. "You've got the whole 'responsible' vibe going on. Anyway, I didn't know how I was going to get away. Didn't even think about it. I just ran."

"Right into me." And he had gotten a real good feel of the body beneath that ugly-ass gown. High, firm breasts, narrow waist, nicely rounded hips. He frowned and shifted as his own body suddenly went tight and uncomfortable. Hell. Just what he needed.

"Yeah, I'm sorry you got dragged into this."

He glanced at her. "No, you're not."

She grinned. "No, I guess I'm really not. Hard to be sorry about finding a white knight."

He let that one go because he was nobody's hero.

"So now what?" he asked. "What are you going to do from here?"

She sat back and stared at him. "I have no idea."

"Well, what was the plan?"

"Like I said, there wasn't a plan. I just had to get away." Shaking her head, she stared out the windshield. "I didn't even know I was going to run until just before I did."

She'd torn down her hair and now it was a tangled mess of dark red curls that flew around her face in the wind whipping through the opened windows. He'd had the AC on, but she'd shut it off and rolled down her window, insisting she needed to feel the wind on her face. Caleb didn't know what it said about him that he preferred that hair of hers wild and free to the carefully pinned-up style she'd had when she ran from the club.

She still had the skirt of her wedding dress hiked up to her knees and Caleb took another admiring look at her long slim legs. Then he fixed his gaze on the road again. "Look, I'll take you out to my ranch—"

"Your ranch."

"That's right."

"Jared said he had a ranch."

Caleb snorted. "The Goodmans used to run a ranch, generations ago. Now they rent the land out to other ranchers so they can live in town."

"So I discovered." She held her hair back, narrowed her eyes on him and asked, "Anyway, we know I'm not crazy."

"Do we?"

She ignored that. "Now I have to ask. Are you a crazy person?"

Both eyebrows lifted and he snorted a laugh. "What kind of question is that?"

"One I probably should have asked *before* I hopped into your truck."

"Good point." A reluctant smile tugged at his mouth.

"Well, I thought I should ask before we go much further down this pretty empty road."

Amused in spite of everything, he asked, "What happened to me being a damn hero rescuing you?"

"Oh, you're still a hero," she assured him, "but you could be crazy, too. You aren't, though, are you?"

"Would I admit it if I was?"

"You might." She shrugged. "There's no telling with crazy people."

"Know a lot of nut jobs, do you?" Caleb shook his head, he couldn't believe he was having this conversation.

"A few, but you don't seem like you're one of them." A wide swath of lace lifted into the wind and she snatched it and held it down on her lap. "Have you ever seen so much tulle?"

"What's tulle?"

"This." She lifted the swath of netting again. "It's awful."

"If you don't like it, Why'd you buy it?"

"I didn't." She sighed. "Jared's mother picked it out." Caleb laughed. "Sounds like her."

"Okay, you're not crazy." She nodded and gave a sigh of satisfaction. "If you don't like my almost mother-in-law you're obviously stable."

"Thanks." Still shaking his head, he said, "Like I was saying, I'll take you to the ranch. You can figure out where to go from there."

"I don't know where I can go," she said quietly turning her head to stare out the window at the scenery flying past. "I don't have my purse, my wallet. God, I don't even have clothes."

Caleb didn't like the sound of the rising hysteria in her voice.

"I don't know what I was thinking," she said, and her words tumbled over each other in their rush to get out. "My God, I don't have anything with me."

"I can take you to an ATM—"

"No purse," she interrupted. "No wallet, remember? No clothes except for this giant marshmallow of a dress." She slapped one hand to her chest as if trying to hold her heart inside her body.

"You're starting to panic," he pointed out.

"Of course I am." Her eyes were wild. "Now that I got away, I can think about other things and what I'm thinking is that I'm alone. In a strange place. Don't know anyone but the people I'm escaping from."

He watched from the corner of his eye as she shook her head frantically.

"I can't exactly go over to the Goodmans' house and say please can I have my things? My clothes. My purse. My ID. My *phone*." She dropped her head into her hands and now her face was covered by what looked like an acre of tulle. "This is a nightmare," she muttered.

"Remember, you wake up from nightmares."

She lifted her head to glare at him. "Easy for you to say since I'm assuming you actually *have* a change of clothing."

"Good point." He nodded. "Yeah, you're about the same size as my sister-in-law. You can wear some of her stuff."

"Great. And what if she doesn't feel like being generous?"

"She's out of town."

A short laugh shot from Shelby's throat. "So I've been on my own about fifteen minutes and already I'm stealing clothes."

"Not stealing. Borrowing." He paused. "Are you always this dramatic?"

"Only when my world implodes," she said and looked at him again. "So basically, I'm homeless and destitute. Well, hasn't this day turned out all sparkly?"

He laughed.

She narrowed her eyes on him, then reluctantly, laughed herself. "This is not how I pictured my life going."

"Yeah, not how I saw my day going, either," he replied, grateful that she seemed to be coming down from that momentary panic.

"Honestly," she said with another shake of her head, "I didn't think beyond moving to Texas to marry Prince Charming who turned out to be a frog."

"And you didn't notice that right off?"

"No." She huffed out a breath and turned her face into the wind. "Usually I'm a terrific judge of character."

When he didn't agree, she reminded him, "I picked *you* to rescue me, didn't I?"

Amused again, Caleb laughed. "Yeah, but your choices were limited."

"I could have just run screaming down the street," she pointed out. "Which was first on my to-do list until I saw you." She paused for breath. "Did you ever notice how appropriate the name Grimm was for an author of fairy tales?"

"Can't say I ever thought about it."

"Well, I've had the time lately. And the motivation. I mean, seriously. Look at this mess. It's got it all. The feckless fiancé who'd gone from hero to wimp. His vicious mother and creepy father, not to mention his grabby brother."

"Grabby?" Caleb scowled at the road ahead and admitted silently that he was really starting to sympathize with his runaway passenger. The Goodman family wasn't exactly the best Royal had to offer and Shelby Arthur had discovered that the hard way.

She shuddered. "Justin is not someone a woman should be alone with. The only bright spot in that family was Jared's sister, Brooke. She must be adopted," Shelby added under her breath, then continued, "but by now, even *she's* probably furious with me."

"Do you need me to respond or are you good to talk all on your own?"

"God this is a mess."

"Seems to be."

She turned to look at him. "Not going to try to console me?"

"Would it do any good?"

"No."

"Then it'd be a waste of time, wouldn't it?"

"Are you always so chatty?" she asked.

"Yep."

Shelby laughed, and the sound was soft and rich and touched something in Caleb he didn't want to acknowledge. Still, her laughter was better than the anxiety he'd just been listening to.

"Look," he said. "You come out to the house and

you can stay there a day or two. Figure out what you want to do."

"Stay there. With you."

He shot her a look. "Don't look so damn suspicious. I'm not offering you a spot in my bed." Damn shame about that, he admitted to himself, since just looking at her made him want to reach out and cover her mouth with his. And a few other things besides. But not the point.

"You can stay on the other side of the house," he said. "My mother died a couple years ago. You can have her wing. We won't even see each other."

"Her *wing*?" Shelby frowned. "How big is this house?"

"Big enough."

At the Texas Cattleman's Club, the reception for the wedding that didn't happen was in full swing. A band played dance music as a Goodman wedding would never have accepted something so pedestrian as a DJ. The tables were decorated with snowy white cloths and a bud vase on each table held a single pink rose. The soft clink of china and crystal was an undercurrent to the music and, while the crowd gathered in knots to exchange gossip about the runaway bride, Rose Clayton sat alone at a table watching it all.

At sixty-seven, Rose was an attractive woman with a figure she took care of, stylishly cut dark brown hair with just a hint of gray—thanks to a talented stylist—that swung in a loose fall at her jawline, and her sharp, smoke-colored eyes never missed a thing.

Conversations rose and fell around her like a continuous wave. She was only half listening, and even at that, she caught plenty of people talking about the upcoming TCC board elections. There had been a time when she wouldn't have given them a thought. But, now that women were also full-fledged members in the Texas Cattleman's Club, she was more than a little interested.

As far as Rose was concerned, their current president, James Harris, was doing a wonderful job and she saw no reason to make a change. It was nice to eavesdrop and hear that most of the other members felt the same way.

As people passed her table, they nodded or smiled, but kept moving. Rose's reputation as the uncrowned queen of Royal society kept people at bay even as they treated her with the respect she'd earned through years of a stubborn refusal to surrender to the unhappiness in her own life.

Rose knew everyone at the reception. She'd watched many of them grow up. Including Margaret Fraser Goodman. The woman, Rose thought, had been *born* an old stick. She had always been more concerned with appearances than with what really mattered. But even as she mentally chastised Margaret, Rose had to admit that she had done the same. The difference was, she assured herself, that Rose found enjoyment within the parameters that had been forced on her so long ago.

Her gaze fixed on Margaret Goodman briefly and noted the crazed look in her eyes and the grim slash of a mouth she kept forcing into a hard smile. Rose had already heard bits and pieces of chatter, no doubt started by Margaret, that had turned the situation around. Now, the story went, it was *Jared* who had changed his mind at the last moment. Told his unfortunate bride to leave.

And a part of Margaret might even believe it. Rose

MAUREEN CHILD   37

had never met the now missing bride, but damn if she didn't admire the woman. She'd taken charge of her own life and done what she'd had to do. Who knew how Rose's life might have turned out if she'd had the same gumption?

But times had been different fifty years ago and Rose's father, Jed, had been a man no one crossed. Her gaze swept the room until she spotted her grandson Daniel. Daniel Clayton was her reward for all of the misery she'd managed to survive over the decades.

A grown man now, he was handsome, intelligent and damned funny when he wanted to be. He was the light of her life and there wasn't a thing she wouldn't do to see him happy. Within reason.

"Oh, that is simply unacceptable," Rose murmured to herself as she saw Daniel bend down and gently kiss a pretty woman who looked dazzled by his attention.

Alexis Slade.

The granddaughter of Gus Slade.

Just thinking the man's name gave Rose's heart a jolt. Once upon a time, she'd been crazy in love with that old goat and risked her father's wrath to be with him. Until the night her father made the threat that had ended everything between her and Gus forever.

She squared her shoulders and lifted her chin. Nodding to people who addressed her, she was a part of the crowd and yet separate from it as her mind raced back through the years.

For decades now, the Claytons and the Slades had been if not enemies, then at least at odds. They didn't socialize. Didn't trust each other. And they surely didn't look at each other as Daniel and Alexis were right that minute. She wouldn't have it. And what's more, Rose was quite sure that on this subject at least, Gus would agree with her.

Their grandchildren had been sweet on each other years ago, but Rose and Gus had put a stop to it. Gus sent Alexis off to an out-of-state college, while Rose kept Daniel so busy with ranch work, he didn't have time to miss the girl he couldn't have.

"Unacceptable," she whispered again, tapping her manicured nails against the tablecloth in a muffled staccato. Again, she scanned the room, but this time, she was looking for someone in particular.

When she found him, Rose stood, crossed the room and stopped at his table. "Gus. We have to talk."

Three

Gus Slade wore a steel-gray suit with a white shirt and a bold red tie. His black cowboy hat rested on the table alongside his arm. His thick hair, once black as midnight, was silver now, and his skin was tanned and leathered from years of working out in the Texas sun. He was leaning back in his chair, one booted foot resting on a knee. At sixty-nine, he was still a powerful, magnetic man.

Damn it.

His piercing blue eyes fixed on Rose with neither welcome nor warning. "Talk about what?"

Ignoring his rudeness, she took a seat near him, glanced over her shoulder toward their grandchildren and said pointedly, *"That."*

He took a look, then frowned. "Nothing to talk about. Keep your boy away from my girl and we have no problem."

"Take another look, you old goat," Rose said in a whispered hush. "It's Alexis doing the flirting. And she's got the look of a woman who's been thoroughly—recently—kissed."

Gus's frown deepened and his gaze shifted to Rose. "A woman flirting doesn't mean a damn thing. And kisses are fleeting, aren't they, Rose?"

She took a gulp of air at the implied insult. Rose had been sixteen years old when she fell head over heels in love with Gus. And if she had to be honest—the man could still give her insides a jump start. But damned if she'd sit there and be insulted.

"I didn't come over here to talk about the past."

"Then why are you sitting at my table?" he snapped.

Rose swallowed back her annoyance. Since the death of his wife, Sarah, from cancer a few years before, Gus had become even more unsociable than usual. And another piece of her heart ached. Sarah Slade had once been Rose's best friend, but Rose had lost them both when she'd rejected Gus. He had turned to Sarah for comfort and soon the two of them had been together, shutting Rose out completely.

But old hurts couldn't matter at the moment. It was the present they had to worry about, not the past. "Gus, unless we're prepared to have the two of them getting together—*again*—we have to come up with something."

He scrubbed one hand across his jaw in a gesture Rose remembered. Deliberately, she shut down a surge of memories and waited impatiently for the man to speak. Gus always had taken his time choosing just the right words. And even back when she had loved him, that particular trait had driven Rose crazy.

"Fine," he said at long last, keeping his voice low as he glanced around to make sure no one could listen in. "But not here. Don't need a damn audience of gossips trying to figure out why we're suddenly being friendly."

Rose winced. She hadn't really considered that. Her one thought had been to enlist Gus's help in breaking up any attachment between her grandson and his granddaughter. "You're right."

He flashed a grin. "Well, this is a banner day. Rose Clayton admitting Gus Slade is right about something."

She was unamused. "Write it on your calendar in big red letters. Meanwhile—"

"Fine, then. We'll meet tomorrow. Two o'clock at the oak."

Rose inhaled sharply at the jab. *The oak* could have been anywhere in the state of Texas. But Rose knew exactly what meeting spot Gus was talking about. She was almost surprised that he remembered. Then, as his gaze focused on her, she realized that he was testing her. Seeing if *she* remembered.

How could she not?

"Agreed. Two o'clock." She turned to walk away, unwilling to give him the satisfaction of seeing that he'd gotten to her. Then she stopped, looked back and said, "Try not to be late this time."

Smiling to herself at the accuracy of her own little barb, Rose walked back to her table.

Shelby stared up at the main house and gave a sigh.

She'd been impressed when Caleb drove through the gates with the scrolled ironwork *M*. Then the oak-lined drive had taken her breath away. But the house itself was amazing.

It was big, sprawling across the ground, like a lazy dog claiming its territory. The house jutted out at different angles that told Shelby people had been adding on to the house for generations. There was a long, wide front porch running the length of the house, with stone pillars holding up the overhang roof.

There were chairs and swings along the length of the porch, crowded with pillows and huge pots filled with flowers spilling down in rivers of bright colors. The effect was a silent welcome to sit and enjoy the view for a while. And the view was pretty spectacular. It was exactly the kind of ranch you would find in a *House Beautiful* article called "The Lifestyles of Rich Ranchers."

She turned in a slow circle, still holding her wedding dress up around her knees. There was a barn, a stable, a corral where three horses were gathered in a knot as if whispering to each other. There was another house, a two-story cottage style just across the yard and in the distance, there were other long, low buildings.

"Wow." She half turned to look up at Caleb. "This is all yours?"

"Mine and my brother's, yeah." He frowned. "Part of your dress is in the dirt."

She looked over her shoulder and muttered a curse. Then she huffed out a breath. "I don't care. Not like I'm going to wear it again. Ever."

He shrugged. "Your call." He pointed to the two-story house. "My brother and his family live there. I'll go get you some of Meg's things."

"I don't know…" It felt weird. She was already so much in his debt, how much deeper could she go? He'd rescued her, offered her a place to stay and now he was going to give her clothes.

"Hey, okay with me if you want to stay in that dress."

Biting her lip, she looked down at the white night-mare she was wearing. "Okay, yes. I'd like to borrow some clothes." *Please don't let him be crazy.*

"Be right back. Oh," he added, "when you go inside, just…watch yourself."

What kind of warning was that? She turned to glance at the wide oak front door and wondered what she was going to find behind it. A torture chamber? Rat-infested rooms? A collection of wedding dresses from the brides he'd rescued before her?

Shelby groaned at that last ridiculous thought. How many brides could one man run across, anyway? After what she'd already been through that day, what in that house could possibly affect her?

So, bracing herself for everything from explosives to bears, Shelby walked across the porch and opened the door.

A blast of icy, air-conditioned air greeted her and she nearly whimpered. She'd thought Chicago summers were killer. But Texas was a brand-new ball game. The humidity here was high enough to fill a swimming pool. Eager to get into the cool, she pushed the door wider but it hit something and stopped.

Curious, Shelby peeked inside and gasped.

Stuff.

Wall-to-wall *stuff.*

The door wouldn't open all the way because there was an antique dresser right in front of it. She didn't need to ask why, either. One step into the main room told Shelby everything she needed to know about Ca-leb's late mother.

The furniture was lovely, but jammed into what

should have been a large, generous room. And on every table, every dresser, every curio cabinet, was stuff. Not old newspapers or magazines, but statues and crystals and rings and bracelets and candlesticks and crystal bowls and baskets and trays.

If Caleb had thought this room would send her screaming, he couldn't have been more wrong. Shelby's organized soul was instantly energized. Her business, Simple Solutions, depended on people like Caleb's mother. Back in Chicago, she'd built her reputation on being able to go into a mess, straighten it out and teach the homeowner how to keep it tidy. Her client list had been built on word of mouth and she was thinking of expanding, hiring more employees, when she'd met Jared Goodman.

Frowning a little, Shelby realized it was hard to believe that she'd given up everything she knew for a man who had ended up being nothing but a facade. She'd trusted him. Believed him. Thought she was in love.

But as it turned out, she'd been in love with the idea of being in love and the reality of actually *marrying* Jared had been enough to jolt her out of the illusion.

Shelby walked farther into the room, lifting one of the crystal bud vases for a closer look, then carefully setting it down again. In her business, she'd learned early about maker's marks on crystal and glass. She knew antiques when she saw them and had a pretty good idea of the value of different pieces.

She did a slow turn, admiring the bones of the room and she wondered why Caleb's mother had felt that emotional need to surround herself with things. The ranch itself was elegant and even in its current state, Shelby could see that the home would be, once cleared out, amazing.

"Yeah, it's pretty bad," Caleb said from behind her.

She turned to look at him. "I've seen worse."

He laughed shortly. "Hard to believe."

"Oh, this is nothing, really." She lifted a porcelain tray and ran her fingertips across the library table it rested on. "No dust. I've been in places where the dust was so thick the furniture looked like ghost pieces. The wood was white with neglect."

"My foreman's wife, Camilla, takes care of things around here."

"Well, she does a good job of it." Shelby looked around again. "It can't be easy to keep all of this dusted."

He sighed and gave a look around. "I keep telling her that we'll get people in here to haul all of this stuff away, but—"

"But you get busy," Shelby said.

"Yeah."

"And that's where I come in."

He turned a wary look on her. "What's that mean?"

"I'm a professional organizer," Shelby said, smiling up at him. "This is what I do. I go into people's homes and help bring order to chaos. I had my own business in Chicago. A successful one."

"And you gave it up to marry Jared," he mused.

"Yes, well." She stopped, frowned. "Bad judgment aside, I'm excellent at what I do." She turned to look at the room again before staring up at him. "I can take care of this for you."

"Is that right?" He was holding a pair of jeans and a T-shirt.

She supposed shoes were too much to hope for.

"Sure. It's great, really." Shelby's mind was racing, figuring, planning and when she had most of it all set, she started talking again. "I need a place to stay for a while."

"Now, wait a second…"

"Just hear me out." She took a breath and released it in a rush. "You've been fabulous. Really. So thanks again for the whole rescue and bringing me here and not being a serial killer."

One corner of his delectable mouth quirked briefly. "You're welcome."

She grinned at him. Really, he was ridiculously good-looking, but when his mouth hinted at a smile, his looks went off-the-chart hot. Still, not the point at the moment.

"But the truth is," she said, "until I can get all of my stuff from Jared's parents' house—not to mention get into my money, I'm stuck."

"What about family?" he asked. "Isn't there someone you could call?"

"No." Sorrow briefly landed on her, gave her a fleeting kiss, then moved on again. "My mother died last year, so I'm all that's left."

"Sorry." He looked uncomfortable.

Shelby understood that, since she'd seen it often back home. So she spoke up quickly to even things out between them again. "Like I said, I'm a professional organizer.

"The plan was to open a business here in Texas…" She frowned, unsure now just what she would do about that. "Back in Chicago, I had hundreds of satisfied clients."

"Uh-huh."

He didn't sound interested, but he hadn't walked away, either. Which meant she hadn't lost him completely. And seeing this house had given her the first shot of good news she'd experienced in days. Before, she'd felt like a beggar, asking for help, borrowing clothes. But if he let her do this, she could feel as though she were paying her way. And that, more than anything, was important to her. She liked being her own boss. In charge of her own life. And right now, she could use a jolt of that in her system.

"My point is," she said eagerly, "I can straighten all of this out for you. I can organize everything of your mother's. All you'll have to do is decide what you want to do with everything."

He glanced around the room again and looked back to Shelby. "It's a big job."

"I'm up to it."

He studied her for a long minute, long enough that she shifted position uncomfortably. What was he seeing when he looked at her? He was seriously gorgeous, so Shelby had to wonder if he was feeling the slightest bit of attraction that was humming through her blood. And the minute she thought it, she pushed it away. *Really? Run away from your wedding and have some completely indecent thoughts about your rescuer? God, Shelby, get a grip.*

"My brother and his wife have already taken what they want, and as for me, keep what works in the room and we could donate the rest of it, I guess," he said.

Concession, her mind shouted and she jumped on it. "Absolutely, and that would be very generous. The crystal alone is probably very valuable. I could contact an antiques store and see about selling some of it if you want me to. I can check all of it for you. Make lists of what you have and where it is and—"

"Do you *ever* stop talking?"

She frowned at him. "Not often. And this is important. I really need to get you to agree with this or I'll be sleeping in a park or something. So I'll do all the work here in exchange for room and board until I can get my life back on track."

"And how long do you figure that will take?"

She winced. "Depends on how cooperative the Goodmans are."

"So forever," he said.

She sighed and felt a momentary dip in her enthusiasm. "I know it's an intrusion on you and I'll try not to bug you much…"

He was watching her and she wished she could read whatever thoughts were digging furrows between his eyebrows. The man was unreadable, though. He was the embodiment of the iconic cowboy. Tall, rugged, gorgeous, stoic. So she was forced to wait. Thankfully, it didn't take long.

"I suppose we could try it."

She sighed, grinned and slapped one hand to her chest. "Thanks. Wow. I feel better already. This is great. You won't be sorry. I'll have this taken care of so fast you won't even recognize the place."

"Uh-huh." He started walking toward the wide hall. "Anyway. You can stay over here in the east wing."

Shelby was looking around the house as she followed him. From what she could see in the hallway, there were plenty of places for her to organize there, too.

"I've never lived in a house with wings."

He glanced down at her as she hurried up to walk

at his side. "Yeah, this one's got all kinds of wings spreading out from here, the center. Every generation has added to it for nearly a hundred and fifty years."

"Wow." Shelby was impressed. She and her mother had been constantly on the move, from apartment to condo, to rental house. They'd never stayed anywhere longer than three years. So hearing about a family who had been in the same spot for more than a century filled her with a kind of envy she hadn't expected. That was roots, she told herself. Digging in, planting yourself and building your own world. One for your children and your children's children.

And that hunger for family, for roots, was what had prompted her to allow herself to be swept off her feet by Jared. Lesson to be learned there, Shelby told herself.

The walls in the house changed from log to stone and back again as they walked. The hardwood floor was shining, letting her know that the house was well cared for in spite of the clutter in the main room that had dribbled into the hallway. She imagined that Camilla had to work like a Trojan to keep everything as clean and beautiful as it was.

Caleb opened a door on the right and stepped inside. Shelby was right behind him, but she stopped on the threshold to simply stare. She gasped because she couldn't help herself. The room was beautiful. Big, with a four-poster cherrywood bed covered by a dark blue-and-white star quilt. There were two end tables, a chest at the foot of the bed and a dresser on the far wall. Two bay windows offered a view of the front yard and the oaks lining the drive.

"This was my mom's room."

Shelby looked at him. "She didn't clutter this one."

"No," he said with a slow shake of his head. "She only did that in the main room and the kitchen. Anyway—" he pointed to a door "—there's a bathroom through there."

"Okay, thanks." Shelby walked farther into the room, laid one hand on the footboard and looked back at Caleb again.

How quickly things turned around, she thought. Only that morning, she'd been in the Goodman family home, dressing for her wedding. She'd felt trapped. Dreading the future she'd set for herself. Boxed into a corner and hadn't been able to see a way out.

Now, hours later, she was in a *real* ranch house with a gorgeous cowboy who'd rescued her from Jared's dragon of a mother. Yeah. Life could turn on you in an instant, so you'd better keep your seat belt on at all times.

"I've got work," he said, dragging her up and out of her thoughts. He tossed his sister-in-law's clothes onto the foot of the bed. "I'll be at the stable or in the first barn."

"Okay." He was so close she could smell the after-shave still clinging to his skin. It was like the woods, she thought. At night. With a full moon. Maybe skinny-dipping in a lake— Okay. She shut her brain off, then blurted, "Just where do *you* sleep?"

"In the west wing," he said. "On the other side of the great room we were in before."

"Oh. Okay." Probably not far enough for her peace of mind, but there wasn't much she could do about it.

One eyebrow lifted. "Problem?"

"No," she said, and then went on because she couldn't tell him that the problem was she was really attracted to him and wanted to see what it would be like to kiss him. Especially since just a couple hours ago, she was supposed to be marrying somebody else. For heaven's sake. It was like she was two people—and one of them was in serious trouble. "You already said you're not crazy and I don't suppose you'll be sneaking over here during the night."

His gaze swept her up and down, then locked on her eyes. "I'll try to control myself."

Frowning, she said, "Well that's flattering, thank you again."

"Do you really need me to tell you that you're beautiful?"

A flush of pleasure snaked through her even as she said, "Of course not."

"Good, because I won't be."

"Is that an insult?"

"Nope. It's a promise." Caleb nodded. "I try not to seduce women wearing wedding gowns. Sends the wrong message." He turned around and headed down the hall. He stopped halfway, looked back over his shoulder and said, "My housekeeper, Camilla, and my foreman, Mike, live in a house behind this one. Out the kitchen door and across the yard. To find the kitchen, just take the main hall straight back."

"Right." She wasn't hungry. Her stomach was still in knots of desperation mingled with relief. But she might go in search of a coffeepot later. And if she was staying—at least temporarily—she would have to meet Camilla and enlist her help. "And, um, thanks. Really."

He nodded and his gaze moved over her again. This time, his inspection was so slow, so thorough, Shelby felt heat flicker to life in her bloodstream.

Seriously, what was wrong with her? She had just

run from one man and now she was getting all fizzy over another one? Maybe this was a breakdown. Some emotional outburst to relieve the tension she'd been living with for weeks.

He shrugged out of his suit jacket and slung it over one broad shoulder, hanging it from the tip of one finger. He tipped his hat back farther on his head and gave her one last, long look. Then he turned and walked away.

His long legs moved slow and easy and Shelby's gaze dropped to his butt. A world-class behind, she thought and swallowed hard. Whatever was happening to her, it hadn't hurt her eyesight any. Dragging in a deep breath, she fought to steady herself and hadn't quite succeeded by the time he disappeared around a corner.

Leaning back against the wall, Shelby sighed a little. *What was it about a cowboy?*

Rose was waiting at the oak the next day when Gus arrived. True to his nature, he was a good fifteen minutes late. Back in another life, when she was young and in love, his tardiness had always irked the hell out of her. But then he'd smile and kiss her and every thought in her head would just melt away.

But that was then.

"You're late."

"And you still like to point out the obvious," Gus said, taking a seat beside her on the bench he had built for the two of them nearly fifty years ago. He slapped one work-worn hand onto the wood, rough from surviving years of wind and rain and sun. "Nice to see this held up."

"You were always good with your hands," Rose agreed.

He glanced at her and one graying black eyebrow lifted. "You used to think so."

She flushed and was surprised by it. Who would have guessed a woman her age was even capable of blushing? Taking a breath, she smoothed her hands across the knees of her khaki slacks and found herself wondering when her hands had aged. How was it the years flew past so quickly?

A lifetime ago, she and Gus would meet here beneath this oak tree. On summer nights, the wind whispered through the leaves, the stars shone down on them like points of flame and it had been as if the two of them were alone in the universe. The present had been exciting and the future looked bright and shiny.

Then it all ended.

Frowning to herself, she looked out over the land. This part of her family ranch hadn't changed much in the last fifty years. There were still cattle grazing in the distance beneath a steely blue sky and the thick canopy of leaves overhead muted the sun's power and lowered the temperature a good ten degrees. And here she was again. With Gus.

"Why did you pick here to meet?"

"Because I knew it would bother you," he admitted with a shrug.

That stung. "At least you're honest about it."

"I put a great value on honesty," Gus said, his voice deep and meaningful as he stared into her eyes. "Always did."

And Rose knew what he was talking about. Once

upon a time, she'd promised to love him forever. Then she'd later turned him away and told him she would never marry him. That she didn't love him and never had. And the lies had cost her, slicing at Rose's soul even as they tore Gus's heart apart while she was forced to watch.

"We're not here to talk about the past," she said, dragging air into tight lungs.

"No, we're damn sure not," he retorted. "So let's get to the point. You tell your grandson to keep his hands off my girl or there's going to be trouble."

Rose laughed shortly. "Don't use that 'lord of all you survey' voice on me. It won't work. And it won't work on Daniel, either." She lifted her chin and met her old lover glare for glare. "My grandson is made of tougher stuff than that. You won't scare him off, Gus, so don't bother trying."

"Well, what the hell do you want me to do, then?" He pushed up from the bench, walked a few feet through the dry brush, then spun about and came back to stand in front of her. "I assume you've got a plan. You always did have more ideas than you knew what to do with."

She sniffed a little, but stood up to meet him on her own two feet. He was still taller than her, but thanks to her Italian-made boots with a two-inch heel, she didn't have to crane her neck to meet his eyes.

"As it happens," she said, "I have been thinking about this."

"And?"

He was irritated and impatient, and she couldn't help but remember that he hadn't always been so anxious to get away from her.

"What we have to do is find each of them some-one else."

"Oh," he said, laughing, "is that all?"

Rose scowled at him. "You might hear me out before you start mocking the whole idea."

"Fine." He folded his arms across his wide chest. "Tell me."

"I was thinking we could do something in Royal. An event. Something big. Something that would attract at-tention not just here, but in Houston, too."

"Uh-huh." Frowning, Gus said, "And what've you got in mind?"

"Well, nothing. Not yet. But you could throw out a few ideas you know." She tapped the toe of her boot against the ground. "This affects both of us, remem-ber?"

"Wouldn't if you could just control your grandson," he muttered.

"Or if you could get your granddaughter to stop look-ing at Daniel with stars in her eyes," Rose countered.

His scowl deepened, but he gave her a grudging nod. "All right. So something that would involve the two of them, but throw them at other people."

"Exactly."

He scrubbed one hand across his jaw and Rose watched him, seeing not just the powerful man he was now, but the man he had once been. The man who'd sto-len her heart when she was only sixteen years old. The man she had thought she'd be with forever.

The man her father had stolen from her.

The irony of this situation wasn't lost on her. Her own father had kept her from the man she loved and now she was scheming to do the same thing to her grandson. But she didn't have a choice. Claytons and Slades were just not meant to be together.

"All right," Gus said, his voice low and deep and somehow intimate. "I'll do some thinking on this, too. We can meet up again in a few days. See what we come up with."

"Fine." She nodded, refusing to acknowledge, even to herself, that she was glad she'd be seeing Gus again.

They stood only a few feet apart, separated by fifty years of mistrust and pain. A soft wind rattled the leaves overhead and pushed through Rose's hair like a touch.

"Well, I've got to be getting back," Gus said abruptly, and Rose jolted as if coming up out of a trance.

"Of course. Me, too."

Nodding, Gus said, "So we meet here again in three days? Same time?"

"That works," she agreed and watched as he turned to walk to his truck. Rose felt a sting of regret, of sorrow and spoke up before she could rethink it. "Gus."

He stopped, turned and asked, "What is it?"

Looking into those eyes that were at once so familiar and so foreign, Rose said something she should have told him two years ago. "I'm sorry about Sarah."

His features went tight, his eyes cool at the reminder of his wife's death. Sarah had once been Rose's best friend, closer than a sister, but Rose had lost her, too, when she had broken things off with Gus. Then lost any chance of reaching out to her at all when she died two years ago.

"Thank you."

Rose took a step closer because she couldn't stand that shut-down look in his gaze. "I should have said something before, but I thought you wouldn't want to hear it from me."

He studied her for several heartbeats before saying softly, "Then you were wrong, Rose."

When he walked away again, she let him go.

Four

For the next couple of days, Caleb did his best to avoid Shelby Arthur. It wasn't easy though because every time he turned around, there she was. She came out to the stables or the barn every so often with a question about one of his mother's "treasures."

He'd been ignoring the problem of his mom's collections since her death a couple of years ago. Hell, with the ranch to run, cattle to see to and the new oil leases to oversee, who had time to clear out furniture? Besides, Caleb didn't know anything about antiques and had no interest in learning.

But now, Shelby was determined to, as she put it, "earn her keep," so he was bombarded with questions daily. She had even enlisted the help of his housekeeper, Camilla, with the job of hauling furniture out to the front porch and covering everything with tarps.

Raina Patterson, the owner of Priceless, the antiques

store at the Courtyard shops in Royal, had already been out to the ranch once. She'd looked everything over and bought a few pieces right away. Soon, there'd be a truck rolling up to take most of it away. But Shelby wasn't half-finished. She was working with Raina to catalog the smaller things Caleb's mother had been hoarding for years.

Caleb already knew his brother, Mitch, wasn't interested in their mother's things, and Meg had taken the few pieces she wanted to remember her mother-in-law by. So the road was clear to clean out the house—and Shelby seemed determined to get it done fast.

Leaning on the rail fence surrounding the corral, Caleb watched the woman working on the front porch of the house. Even from across the yard, Caleb felt that hot zip of something tantalizing shoot through his blood and settle in his groin. Shelby was still wearing Meg's jeans, and they were a little tight on her, which worked fine for him. She'd also asked Caleb for a couple of his T-shirts, and she was wearing one of them now.

The shirt was way too big, but she'd fixed that by tying it off under her breasts so that her midriff was bare and he could admire that swath of tanned skin and daydream about seeing more of her. Her curly auburn hair was pulled up into a ponytail that danced across her shoulders, and the wedding sandals she wore looked both out of place and enticing on her long, narrow feet.

Caleb gritted his teeth as Shelby bent in half to tug a table out the front door. Her butt looked good in those faded jeans and he'd give a lot to see it naked. To touch it. To stroke down the curves of her body and then to—

"She's a hard worker, you gotta give her that."

Squeezing his eyes shut briefly, Caleb willed away

the tightness in his jeans and turned his head to watch his foreman, Mike Taylor, walk up to join him.

"Yeah, she's busy enough. Driving me nuts with all the questions, though."

"I can see that," Mike allowed, bracing both arms on the top fence rail. "But gotta tell you, Cam's happy as hell that Shelby's getting all that extra furniture out of the house. She's been grumbling about keeping it all dusted and clean."

Caleb nodded and turned his eyes back to Shelby. She'd moved on from tugging the furniture outside and now she was stretching to cover it all with yet another tarp. Of course, stretching like she was bared more of her midriff and had her extending one leg out like a ballet dancer.

Clearing his mind of every wicked thought currently gleefully tormenting him, he said only, "Will be nice to be able to walk through that room again."

"Uh-huh." Mike glanced at him, then grinned when he followed Caleb's gaze. "She's a good-looking woman."

"And you're a married man."

"Don't make me blind," Mike said, grinning. "Couldn't help but notice you noticing her."

"Is that right?" Caleb pushed off the fence and stuffed both hands into his jeans pockets. "If you've got so much extra time to spend 'noticing' things, maybe we should find you more work."

"You could do that," Mike said, teasing tone still in his voice, letting Caleb know he wasn't the least bit intimidated. "Or you could admit that woman's got you thinking."

"What I'm thinking is, we need to call the vet back out to check on the mare again."

"Yeah. You know, Cam tells me Shelby's not only beautiful, but she's smart, too. Hell, she has to be. Got herself out of marrying Jared Goodman."

"Got herself *into* it, too," Caleb reminded him. And in spite of the attraction he felt for her, that was the one thing that kept nibbling at his mind. Yeah, she was gorgeous and had a body that haunted him day and night. God knew she could talk the ears off a statue. And she wasn't afraid of work, so that was another point for her.

But bottom line was, she'd run out on her own wedding and left her groom—even if it was Jared Goodman—standing at the altar looking like a fool.

And that hit way too close to home for Caleb. He'd been in Jared's position and he knew firsthand just how hard it was. Yes, Meg had run off the night before their wedding, so Caleb hadn't actually been caught standing in front of a roomful of people looking like a jackass. But close enough. How in the hell could he be with a woman who had done to a man what had been done to *him*?

Caleb had been keeping his finger on what was going on in Royal over the failed wedding. The Goodmans were handling all of this a lot differently than he had, of course. They'd spun the story around until Jared was a damn hero who'd cut a gold digger loose before she could marry him.

Shelby hadn't heard any of that yet and he had a feeling she'd be furious when she inevitably did. Most people in Royal weren't buying the story, but enough folks were that he'd heard all kinds of ugly rumors about Shelby when he'd gone into town the day before.

And though a part of him wanted to defend her, he'd kept quiet because hell, he didn't even *know* the woman who'd taken up residence in his house. All he knew for sure was that he wanted her more than he'd ever wanted anyone and he couldn't have her.

"True enough," Mike concurred. "She did agree to marry him. But the important part is, she was smart enough to see the mistake before she made it permanent."

Caleb turned his head to look at his friend. "And that makes it okay?"

Mike frowned, squinted into the afternoon sun and shook his head. "Didn't say that, Boss. But you've got to admit this situation isn't like yours was."

He hated it. Hated that everyone knew what had happened and could drag it up and toss it at him when he least expected it. But memories were long in Royal.

"This isn't about me."

"Isn't it?" Mike smiled now. "I've seen the way you watch her." He laughed a little. "Hell, like you were watching her a minute ago—until she went back in the house."

Caleb shot his friend a hard look. "Since when is looking at a pretty woman a crime?"

"Since never. Yet, anyway," he added. "I'm just saying, she's single, you're single—what the hell, Boss?"

"It's complicated and you know it."

"I know you can untangle any knot if you want to bad enough."

Caleb ground his teeth together, took a long, deep breath and said, "Don't you have somewhere to be? Something to do?"

"Sure do. Just came over to tell you Scarlett's coming over later to give the mare another checkup."

Scarlett McKittrick was the town vet and there was

nobody better with every animal—from puppies to cows to stallions. "Fine. Let me know when she gets here."

"You got it. Hey…" Mike jerked his head toward the long, oak-lined drive. "What's the sheriff doing here?"

Caleb turned his head and watched Nathan Battle's black Suburban approach the house. "Guess I'd better find out."

Rather than walk around and go through the gate, Caleb hopped the fence and was waiting when Nate brought his car to a stop and parked opposite the ranch house front door. The sun was hot, the air was still and dripping with humidity. And the look on Nate's face promised trouble.

"Hey, Caleb," he said as he climbed out of the car. "Shelby around?"

"Yeah. She's in the house. What's this about, Nate?"

Nathan tugged his hat off, swept one hand through his hair and grimaced. "The Goodman family's making some noise about suing Shelby."

"What?" Behind him, the front door opened, slammed shut and Shelby's quick footsteps sounded out in the stillness.

She moved up to stand beside Caleb and he could have sworn he felt heat pumping from her body into his. Probably just the Texas sun—or at least that's what he was going to tell himself.

"They're going to sue me?" she asked, dumbfounded.

"Didn't say that, miss," Nate told her, turning his hat in his hands. "Said they're making noises about it."

"Sue me for what?"

Caleb was interested in hearing that, too.

"Well, miss," Nate winced and looked as though he

wished he were anywhere but there. "They say defamation of character. That you've made Jared look bad in his hometown."

Caleb snorted. "Jared's looked bad since he was in grade school."

Giving Caleb a wry smile, Nathan nodded. "I know that, but his mother sure doesn't seem to."

"They can't sue me," Shelby whispered and turned her gaze up to Caleb. "Can they?"

Why in the hell he would feel like protecting her, he couldn't say. But there it was. In the couple of days he'd known her, he'd seen fight and spirit and joy and relief in her eyes. He didn't much care for the worry he saw there now.

"They can," he said firmly, "but they won't."

"I wish I could believe that," she said softly.

Nate and Caleb exchanged a long look that Shelby saw. "What? What is it you two know that I don't?"

Giving a sigh, Caleb turned to her. "To Margaret Goodman, the only thing that matters is how something *looks* to someone else. It's all about appearances with her. Margaret's not going to drag Jared into a court battle where every woman in town would testify on your behalf that he's a weasel and you were smart to back out."

"Oh, God. I'm sort of relieved and a little horrified." Taking a step backward, Shelby kept moving until the backs of her knees hit a rocking chair, then she dropped into it. "How could I have been so stupid?"

Caleb almost answered, then he realized she was talking to herself, complete with wild hand gestures and shakes of her head that sent her ponytail swinging like a pendulum in a tornado. All he could do was stand there and listen.

"I never saw it," she muttered. "But truthfully, I didn't want to see it, either. I wanted the fantasy. He said he was a cowboy. Who could turn down a cowboy?"

"Is she all right?" Nate asked, a worried frown etched into his forehead.

"Damned if I know," Caleb admitted, watching the woman as she continued her private rant. He thought maybe he should say something, but then she might not even hear him. She wasn't really paying any attention to him and Nate at all. It was as if she were all alone and she was having a good argument. With herself.

"He said he had a ranch, but he doesn't have a ranch. He's a *lawyer.* And he's afraid of his *mother.* But then, everyone's afraid of her. I was, wasn't I?"

"Shelby…" Caleb wasn't sure she could hear him.

She shook her head even harder and that dark red ponytail went swinging again. "Was I really that stupid? Or just lonely? He was cute, sure, but I think I just wanted to be in love so badly that I purposely didn't see what I should have seen if I'd been really looking, you know?"

"Uh…" Nate was still watching her as if she might explode. "Is she actually talking to us?"

"I don't think so," Caleb mused.

"Texas is so different from home, but I thought that would be a good thing, but is it? Oh, no. So now I don't even have any extra *underwear* and they want to sue me? How is that fair?"

Talking to Caleb, even while he kept a wary eye on Shelby, Nate said, "I did manage to get her purse back from Mrs. Goodman—"

"My *purse*?" Shelby shot from the chair and snatched it from Nate's hand as soon as he pulled it out of his truck. She clutched the big, brown leather bag to her chest like a beloved child. Then she glanced inside. "Oh, my wallet. And my phone and lip gloss and my knife…"

"You have a knife?" Caleb asked.

"Doesn't everyone?" Shelby retorted, pulling a small Swiss Army knife out to hold up and show them. Then she looked past Nate toward his car as if she could find what she was looking for. "But what about the rest of my stuff? My suitcases? My clothes? Shoes?"

Nate grimaced. "Margaret says she's holding on to them for now."

"What?" She looked up at him. "Why?"

"Pure cussedness, I'd guess," Caleb muttered. Nate caught his comment and nodded.

"That's what it looks like to me, too."

"I have *one* pair of underwear," she snapped. "I can't live like that. Nobody could."

Nate's expression went from concerned to embarrassed and back again. But Caleb wasn't thinking about Nate. It was Shelby who had his full attention.

The disappointment on her face tore at Caleb. In the last couple of days, she'd been hanging on, doing what she had to, to cling to whatever part of her world was left. She'd been working hard the last few days, making sense of his late mother's collections and trying to bring some order to the house. It hadn't been easy.

And hell, Caleb could admit, at least to himself, that he hadn't helped any. He'd avoided her, ignored her presence as best he could, since the mere thought of her was enough to tighten his body to painful levels.

Hell, he was no fan of Jared Goodman, but he felt for the man. Caleb had been in Jared's position and it was hard to let go of that. But at the same time, he had to admit that Shelby had done what she thought was right. Had made a decision that couldn't have been an easy one and now she was still paying for it.

"Give Margaret a couple days to cool off some. I'll get your things back for you," Nate said in a soothing tone that seemed to ease some of the tightness from Shelby's features.

She smiled at Nate, then looked up at Caleb. He saw the shine in her eyes and hoped to God she wasn't going to cry. He hated it when women cried. Always left him feeling helpless, something he wasn't accustomed to.

She blinked the tears back, forced a smile he knew she wasn't feeling and said, "Well, at least I have my purse. I can go shopping for clothes and—"

"Yeah." Nate sighed and said, "About that. You'll have to use a credit card. Apparently Jared took you off the joint bank account, so your ATM card won't work."

"He can't do that," she argued, and all hints of tears evaporated in a rush of fury. "All of the money I got from the sale of my house is in that account. It's *my* money."

Caleb dropped one hand onto her shoulder and he felt her tremble. But he had the distinct impression that tremor was caused by pure rage. He couldn't blame her for it.

"Nate," Caleb said, "they can't do that. It's the same as stealing."

"You think I don't know that?" Shaking his head, the sheriff looked at Shelby. "I've already spoken to the judge and she says if you have proof of the deposit you made, she'll release the money to you."

"Do you?" Caleb asked. "Have proof, I mean."

"I do, but the problem is, it's in my suitcase." Her

shoulders slumped in defeat. "And the suitcase is at the Goodmans' house."

"I'll go over there," Caleb said. "Get her things."

"You'll stay out of it," Nate warned, aiming a steely look at Caleb. "Margaret's already half-convinced that *you're* the reason Shelby ran out on Jared."

"Me?" He was honestly stunned.

"Him?" Shelby echoed.

Caleb scowled at Nathan. "How the hell did Margaret come to that?"

"Shelby ran from the wedding straight to you." Nate shrugged helplessly. "You drove off with her. Now she's living here in your house."

Caleb bit back a curse. Damn it, he'd spent the last four years trying to live down a rich gossip vein and now he'd opened himself up to a brand-new one. Royal would be buzzing and though it was irritating as hell, it didn't really bother him as much as he would have expected it to.

Maybe it was because Shelby was standing there beside him looking outraged. Her eyes were flashing and there were twin spots of color in her cheeks. A hot Texas wind kicked up out of nowhere and sent those dark red curls of hers flying and all in all she made a picture designed to bring a man to his knees.

"But that's ridiculous," Shelby argued. "All he did was *help* me."

"Doesn't matter to Margaret," Nate said, then turned his attention back to Caleb.

"Yeah, I don't care what Margaret Goodman has to say and most people in Royal feel the same." Not completely true. He did hate the thought of being the subject of speculation and more gossip. But he didn't give a good damn what Margaret Goodman thought of him. Caleb looked at Shelby. "Whatever gossip springs up around this won't last long." He hoped. "The town's wagging tongues will move on to something more interesting."

"Just keep your distance from the Goodmans," Nathan said. "I'll go talk to Simon. See what I can do about getting your things, Shelby. If I have trouble with it, we can always email your bank and have them send you a copy of everything."

"Right. Okay. Yes. Good idea. Thanks I can do that. I'll do it tomorrow. Just in case." She kept nodding and Caleb figured it was just reaction. A hell of a lot of information dumped on her in just a couple of minutes. And not much of it was good.

He couldn't help but wonder what she was thinking. Her eyes gave nothing away, but thankfully they weren't filled with unshed tears anymore, either. And he had to admit it was worrying how quiet she'd gotten all of a sudden. He'd become used to her just talking his ears off.

He glanced at his friend. "Thanks, Nate."

"Sure. I'll be in touch. Shelby," he added, "we'll get this all straightened out."

She only nodded at him, making Caleb wonder again. He never would have believed he'd actually *miss* her rambling conversations and monologues.

The sheriff got back in his car and drove away, leaving the two of them alone on the porch.

Shelby was still petting that brown leather bag lovingly and holding it as if it were a life vest keeping her afloat in a churning sea. She didn't say anything, but Caleb could guess what she was thinking. Her world was a damn mess and for a woman with an organized soul like Shelby, that had to be hard to take.

"Well," she finally said with a shrug, "I guess I should get back to work."

No complaints. No cussing. No kicking the porch railing in sheer frustration. Just acceptance and moving on. Damned if Caleb didn't admire her. Shelby Arthur was an impressive woman. She'd had the world tipped on her again and she wasn't letting it drag her down. He'd never known anyone who bounced back from bad news as quickly and completely as she did. Maybe that was why he heard himself make an offer he hadn't planned on. "The work can wait."

"What? Why?" She looked up at him, so he was staring into her eyes when he spoke again.

"How about I take you shopping?"

The flash of pleasure in those green eyes of hers stirred simmering embers inside him into blistering hot coals that threatened to immolate him.

It would be a hell of a burn.

Five

Caleb didn't take her to Royal and Shelby was grateful. She knew the small town was still gossiping about her and that catastrophe of a wedding. If they'd been in Royal, everyone would have been staring. Whispering. There was already talk and if people had seen the two of them together, that would have only fueled the fire. Not to mention there would have been a chance of running into some of the Goodman family.

But in Houston, no one knew her. No one cared that she and Caleb were walking together down a busy street. The only people looking at them were women, taking quick, approving glances at Caleb. He didn't seem to notice, but Shelby did. And if truth be told, she'd been sending him quite a few of those glances herself.

He was wearing black jeans and boots, a white shirt with a black blazer tossed over it. That gray hat he always wore was pulled down low on his forehead, shadowing his eyes and making him look…fantastic. The man was so sexy, her imagination was constantly fueled just by the thought of him.

There. She'd admitted it to herself. Caleb Mackenzie was like a walking sex dream. That slow drawl of his rumbled along a woman's skin like a touch and when his eyes fixed and held on her, Shelby felt as though he was looking right down into her soul. It was a little unsettling and at the same time thrilling in a way she'd never known before. Then there were the boots. And his long legs and the way jeans clung to them. His chest was broad and his hands were big and calloused from years of hard work and she really wanted to know what those hands felt like on her skin.

Then, as if he wasn't already droolworthy, there was the shopping. He could have gone to a bar or something to wait for her, but he'd walked with her. Kept her company and offered opinions—whether she wanted them or not—on the clothes she'd purchased. The only time he'd left her alone was in the lingerie department and she wished he had stayed. Having him watch while she picked out bras and underwear would have been…exciting. Which was just ridiculous, she lectured herself. She had no business fantasizing about *another* cowboy so soon after turning her whole world inside out for a would-be cowboy.

Shelby slapped her forehead. She must be losing her mind. Had to be the strength of the Texas sun broiling down and baking her brain.

"Is there a reason you're hitting yourself in the head?"

She glanced up at him and instantly, her stomach did

a flip-flop and her heartbeat skittered a little. Not that she could tell him that. Heatstroke. That had to be it.

"Um, no," she said. "Just wishing I'd picked up a pair of sandals at the last store."

Oh, good one.

He shook his head. "The ones you bought aren't enough?"

"Right. Right." Idiot. Really. She *had* bought a pair of sandals. God, she was a terrible liar.

The sidewalk was bustling. Businessmen, teenagers, women out with friends to do some window-shopping or just hurrying to work. The city was loud and crowded and the sizzling sun ricocheted off the cement and slammed back into you just for the hell of it. And Shelby was loving every minute.

In the month or so she'd been in Texas, she'd gotten used to the small town feel of Royal, and she loved it, really. But there was an excitement and a buzz about being in a big city and a part of her had missed it. Especially right this minute.

She was wearing a brand-new dress that was sky blue, summer weight with spaghetti straps and a full skirt that fell to just above her knees. The three-inch taupe heels she wore with it were perfect and it was good to feel…pretty, again. She was so tired of borrowed jeans and T-shirts.

"Most big cities are pretty much alike you know," she said, pitching her voice to be heard over a blasting car horn.

"That right?"

"Well, that's what I've heard people say. And I actually believed it until today. I thought, how different can

Houston be from Chicago?" She grinned. "Turns out, *very* different."

"The hats?" he asked, showing off the half smile that turned her insides into jelly all too briefly.

"Oh, absolutely," she said, "but it's more than that, too. Houston's busy and loud and people are racing around to get somewhere else. But even with all that, it's more...relaxed. More, casual somehow."

Caleb stepped out of the way of a businessman in a hurry and steered Shelby to one side with his hand at the small of her back.

She took a breath and held it. It didn't mean anything, she knew. It had been just a simple, polite gesture. Yet, the touch of his hand sent arrows of heat dipping and diving through her body. Her physical reactions to him were getting stronger, harder to ignore.

Every time they were anywhere near each other, it felt like a fuse had been lit and sparks were flying. She couldn't be sure if he felt it, too, but she was guessing he did because he was actively ignoring her. And she'd let him, figuring it was best all the way around.

After all, she was just out of one relationship and she wasn't looking for another. But no matter how much she ignored Caleb during the day, her dreams were full of him. Every time she closed her eyes, there he was. It seemed her subconscious was all too eager to explore possibilities.

"I want to say thank you again, for everything, but it feels like I'm always thanking you," she said abruptly in an attempt to drag her mind out of the bedroom.

"Yeah, you don't have to." He took her arm and steered her around yet another businessman—this one in an ill-fitting suit yelling into his cell phone, oblivious to anyone else on the sidewalk.

"Thanks," she said, then added, "oops."

His mouth quirked and Shelby silently congratulated herself. Honestly, when she coaxed that half smile out of the man she felt as if she'd been awarded a prize.

"This is great," she said, clutching two bags from local shops. "And oh, boy, am I looking forward to wearing fresh underwear. It's really a pain washing my one pair out every night and hanging them on a towel bar to dry. I was afraid I was going to wear out the fabric."

Okay, probably shouldn't be talking about her underwear.

"And shoes. I love my shoes. Especially those boots we found. I feel very Texan," she said, rattling the bag containing the boots.

"I don't think you can call hot-pink cowboy boots *Texan*."

"I bought them here, so... Texas."

"You bought *everything* here," he mused, holding up the three bags he was carrying.

She thought about everything in the shopping bags and smiled to herself, though she knew that when her credit card showed up, she'd probably have a heart attack. But that was a worry for another day. At least she didn't feel homeless *and* clothesless anymore. Her world was still up in the air. Her ex-about-to-be-mother-in-law was still making trouble for her. She couldn't touch any of her own money, but damn it, she had new underwear.

"I really love this," she said, looking around the busy street and the high-rises surrounding them. "It's nice, getting away from Royal for a while."

"The city's all right, once in a while," he agreed, frowning when a bus stopped at the sidewalk and belched out a cloud of dark smoke. "But Royal's better, even if small towns are hard to take sometimes."

"Oh, I like the town and most of the people I've met but I hate knowing they're talking about me. I mean, back in Chicago, I was just a face in the crowd." She looked around at the city and the thousands of people. "Like I am here. I wanted the small town life, you know? Roots. Home. Family. That's mostly why I agreed to marry Jared, I think. I wanted it so badly, I didn't notice that the man offering it to me wasn't real. Wasn't worth it."

A woman pushed past them, shoving Shelby into Caleb and he took her arm to steady her before letting her go again. "Was it really so important to you?"

"Spoken like a man who's always had a home. A place." They stopped at the corner and she laid one hand on his forearm. "My mother raised me on her own after my father died. We were happy, but we never stayed. Anywhere."

Caleb's eyes met hers and she kept talking, wanting him to understand why she'd done what she had. "I always wanted a real home, you know? A place where people would know me, where I'd belong." Her hand dropped away and she looked past him, at the busy street. "When Jared came along, I think I convinced myself I loved him because I *did* love what he represented."

A sea of people walked past them, and neither of them moved—or even noticed.

"Why'd you wait till the last minute to walk out?" Caleb watched her, waiting for her reply. "You were in Royal a month before the wedding."

"I know." She sighed and started walking again. In her heels, they were nearly eye to eye when she glanced at him. Caleb moved up alongside her. The sun was hot on her back and she was squinting against the glare. In the bustle and noise of the city, she kept talking. "I felt... trapped. I'd said yes already and so I let Jared's mother steamroll me. It was easier to go along than to try to stop what I had put into motion, you know?"

"Not really," he said.

She gave him a wry smile. "Yeah, I don't really understand it now, either. But the day of the wedding, I just suddenly *knew* I couldn't go through with it. Couldn't let one lie become a lifetime lie. So I ran."

She glanced at him and was relieved to see him nod as if he got it, though his mouth was a grim line. Shelby didn't know why she cared what Caleb Mackenzie thought of her, but she did. Talking about the wedding, the Goodman family, all brought back what the sheriff had said to her earlier and as his words replayed in her mind, she worriedly chewed at her bottom lip. Shelby hadn't wanted to make a big deal about it at the time, but the more she thought about it, the more nervous she felt. "What if the Goodmans do sue me?"

"They won't."

She wished she felt as sure as he sounded. "We don't know that."

"Yes, we do." He stopped at an intersection along with what seemed like half the city as they waited for the light to change. Caleb glanced down at her and though his eyes were shadowed by the brim of his hat, she could read the reassurance there. "Simon Goodman's a lawyer—and honestly, not all that good a one.

He's not going to start up a court case he's not sure he can win."

Sounded reasonable. And yet… "But like you said. Small town, people know him and don't know me, why wouldn't he win?" Shelby smiled at a baby in a stroller.

"Mainly because people *do* know him," Caleb told her as the light changed and they moved with the herd. "Know him and don't much like him."

"Isn't he *your* lawyer?" Shelby hurried her steps to keep up with his much longer stride. Even on a crowded sidewalk, Caleb walked like a man with a purpose. Determined. Unstoppable. Was there anything sexier? *Back on track, Shelby.* "I mean, Cam told me that's why you were at the wedding in the first place."

"Yeah," he admitted. "He is and that's my fault. He was my father's lawyer. I just never changed. Should have. Just got busy."

"Wow. Five sentences in a row."

"What?"

"The stoic cowboy spoke—almost at length," she said, tipping her head up to look into his eyes. It was weird, but now that she'd told him why she'd come to marry Jared and why she hadn't, she felt…free. Shelby had never been good with secrets. They always came back to bite her in the butt. So having the truth out there and Caleb's seeming understanding, lifted a weight off her shoulders.

He looked down at her and his mouth quirked again. Score.

"I must be a good influence on you," she said, giving him a wide smile. "I bet until I came around, nobody at the ranch talked much."

"Nobody comes close to you, that's for damn sure," he muttered.

"Isn't that nice?" He didn't mean it as a compliment but she was taking it as one. When he smiled again, as if they were sharing the joke, Shelby's heart gave a quick flutter.

"Caleb!" A feminine voice called his name and beside her, Shelby sensed him flinch in reaction.

They stopped, let the pedestrian crowd flow past, and then Shelby watched what was left of the crowd part, like a scene from a movie, to allow a drop-dead-gorgeous woman rush forward.

Her hair was long and blond, her eyes were blue and she wore a sleek, black dress that hugged every voluptuous curve. Black heels completed the outfit and Shelby, despite her pretty new dress and shoes, suddenly felt like a country bumpkin. Whatever that was.

"Caleb, you look fantastic!" The blonde hurled herself into Caleb's arms and even Shelby caught the cloud of floral scent that clung to her.

"Marta," Caleb said, extricating himself as gently as possible. "Good to see you."

To Shelby, it looked as though he was trying to get away from an octopus and he didn't look very happy about it. Which really made her feel better. Although why this little scene should bother her at all was beyond her. She and Caleb weren't a thing. She'd only known him a short time. And yet…logic didn't seem to have a lot to do with what she was feeling at the moment.

"God, it's been forever," Marta exclaimed, stepping back, but keeping a tight grip on one of Caleb's hands as if afraid he might try to escape.

"Yeah," he said, "I've been busy."

She playfully slapped at his chest. "You and those cows of yours."

"Cattle," he corrected, but Marta obviously didn't care.

"How long are you in the city for?" She gave her hair a playful toss and pouted prettily. All the while continuing to ignore Shelby's presence completely. "We've got to have dinner, Caleb, do some catching up. You can come to my place and—"

"Sorry can't do it," Caleb said, interrupting the flow of words and startling Marta into temporary silence.

Caleb looked down at Shelby. "We've got to be getting back, isn't that right, darlin'?"

Stunned, Shelby could only stare into those icy-blue eyes of his. His gaze was fixed on hers and she could see that he wanted her to play along with him. For his own reasons, he wanted to get rid of Marta and that worked for Shelby. She smiled, letting him know that she was on board, ready for whatever he had in mind. Briefly, he let his forehead rest against hers as if in solidarity.

"That's right, honey," she said softly.

Smiling then, Caleb draped his free arm around her shoulders, pulled her in tight to his side and dropped a kiss on top of her head. "Shelby, honey, this is Marta. An old friend."

"Really. How old?" she asked innocently, and watched Marta's eyes flash and narrow.

"Marta, this is Shelby and we're together now, so…"

The blonde gave Shelby a quick inspection and judging by the look in her eyes, wasn't impressed. Then Shelby wrapped her arm around Caleb's waist and rested her head against his chest in a clearly proprietary gesture. A few seconds later, the blonde surrendered.

"Well, all right, then, if that's how it is."

"Good to see you, though," Caleb said.

"And I just love meeting my honey's old friends," Shelby added, snuggling in even closer to Caleb.

"Yes, I can see that," Marta said, amused now. "Well, you two enjoy your day in the city. Caleb, you've got my number if things change."

"They won't be changing," Shelby assured her. A part of her really wished that were true.

"Right. Well, I'll be getting along to my lunch appointment. Still, it was good to see you, Caleb."

"Yeah. You, too."

Marta walked away and they watched her go. Caleb's arm was still around Shelby's shoulders as she tipped her face up to look into his eyes. "You know those boobs are fake, right?"

He laughed and gave her a hard squeeze before letting her go. "You can trust me on this. They're real."

"Hmm." People streamed past them like a creek rushing past rocks in its way. "You know what? After all this shopping, the least I can do is buy you a late lunch. Or an early dinner." She glanced around. "Is there a diner or a burger place around here?"

Caleb shook his head. "I think we can do better than that."

"Mr. Mackenzie," the hostess at the Houston Grille said, giving him a wide smile. She had jet-black hair cut into a wedge that hugged her cheekbones. "Good to see you again."

"Thanks, Stella," Caleb replied, looking into the main dining room. Windows fronting on the busy street boasted dark red awnings over them, giving the diners a nice view without being blinded by the sun. The atmosphere was muted, with weeping violins at a whispered volume pumped through speakers mounted discreetly on the walls. Tables were covered with white linen and the waitstaff moved across the floor like ballet dancers, with grace and efficiency. "Is my regular booth available?"

"It sure is." She picked up two menus, smiled at Shelby and then stopped when Caleb asked her to keep their shopping bags for them. Once they were stowed, Stella preceded them to a booth with a wide view of downtown Houston.

Shelby slid across the maroon leather bench seat and Caleb followed right after. "Can we get a couple of iced teas as soon as possible?"

Stella said, "Right away," and moved off.

Shelby's eyes were wide as she took in the restaurant before turning to him. "This place is beautiful."

"Why are you whispering?"

She laughed and he wondered why the sound of it should affect him as much as it did.

"It feels like I should. Everything is so dignified and well, quiet."

"You'll have to come back on a Saturday night. It's a lot louder then." He nodded to the waiter who brought them their drinks, then looked at Shelby again. She really was beautiful. That new dress of hers hugged her figure and highlighted everything he wanted to touch.

"This has been a really terrific day, Caleb. Thanks for bringing me."

"Stop saying thank you."

She shrugged, took a sip of her tea and set it back down again. "If you want me to stop saying it, then you need to stop doing nice things for me."

A waiter came to the table then. "Are you ready, Mr. Mackenzie?"

Turning to Shelby, he asked, "How hungry are you?"

"Very."

"Okay. Trust me with the order?"

She looked at him and those grass-green eyes fascinated him as they always did. "Sure."

Nodding, he looked at the waiter. "We'll each have the strip steak, rare. Cheese potatoes and the bacon asparagus."

"Right away." The waiter hurried off and Caleb looked back to Shelby.

"Is there anything else you want to buy while we're in the city?"

"No," she said, her fingers delicately tracing the prongs of the sterling silver fork in front of her. "This will do me until I get my own clothes back from the Goodmans." She looked at him. "How much longer do you think?"

Irritation spiked. Caleb had been raised to do the right thing. Always. To have the Goodmans treating Shelby this way, holding back her property from her, just for spite, annoyed the hell out of him. Especially since Nate was convinced that if Caleb did anything, he'd only make the situation worse.

Caleb didn't much care for *waiting*.

"No telling, really," he finally answered. "But Nate's a good man and an even better sheriff. He'll take care of this and get it all sorted out as soon as he can."

"That's good," she said.

"I hear a *but* in there," Caleb pointed out, his gaze fixed on her. The woman held his attention no matter what she was doing. And now her eyes looked anxious and the way she was chewing at her bottom lip sent tugs of heat to his groin even while he wondered what the hell she was worried about.

She smiled. "*But*, I can't just stay at your ranch forever. That's not right. I'm nearly finished clearing out your mother's collection and when that's done…"

He didn't want her to leave. What the hell? Caleb told himself it was because he was used to having her around. But the truth was more unsettling. He simply *wanted* her. There. In his house. In his bed. Under him. Over him.

He wanted Shelby Arthur like nothing else ever in his life.

But he could hardly admit to that. "Don't worry about it," he said dismissively. "Stay as long as you need to. There's plenty more in the house that could use organizing. Talk to Cam about it. In fact, have her show you the attic when you're finished with the kitchen and great room."

"The attic?"

"There are things up there dating back more than a hundred years." This was, at least, the truth. "It'd be good to get it sorted out, with the family papers and such filed properly."

Her eyes gleamed and he smiled to himself. The woman was hell on wheels when it came to straightening things out. Heck, if it kept her in his house, he'd create new chaos somewhere.

"Hey, Caleb."

He turned and smiled, holding out one hand to the man greeting him. Reese Curran, best horse trainer Caleb had ever seen and now married to Lucy Navarro Bradshaw. Just a few months ago, Reese had come home to Royal and it hadn't taken long for he and Lucy to find each other again. It was good to see Lucy happy again. "Reese. Nice to see you. Lucy," he added, with a nod to the woman standing beside the tall, lanky cowboy.

"I'm so glad to see you," Lucy said, then turned her gaze to Shelby and held out one hand. "You must be Shelby. Good to finally meet you."

"Thanks."

"Shelby, this is Reese and Lucy Curran. They run a horse rescue operation at Paradise Farms, on the McKittrick ranch. Not far outside of town." Caleb looked at his friend. "So what're you two doing in the city?"

"Shopping," Lucy crowed, with a grin as she wrapped an arm around her husband's waist to give him a squeeze.

"Lot of that going around," Caleb mused with a sly smile at Shelby. She grinned back at him and a fork of heat sliced right through him.

"Yes, but we're shopping for maternity clothes," Lucy said with a delighted smile.

"Well, congratulations." Caleb shook Reese's hand again, then pushed out of the booth to give Lucy a quick hug. He'd known Lucy's family his whole life, so Lucy was like a little sister to him. He'd watched her suffer when she'd lost her first husband, the father of her boy, Brody. He'd seen her worry over her brother Jesse and her step-brother Will when they'd recently tackled some hard family issues. And he'd celebrated with her when she and Reese had found each other not too long after Jesse and Will had both found loves of their own.

"That's wonderful," Shelby said as Caleb settled back into the booth.

"It really is," Lucy agreed. "And it's one more reason

I'm glad to meet you. Cam told me what a whiz you are at organizing things. I'd really like you to come out to the ranch and take a look at our plans for the new house Reese is building. Brody needs a big-boy space all his own and I'd love to get your opinions on what to do for the baby's room."

Eyes sparkling at the idea of a new challenge, Shelby said, "I'd love to."

"Great." Lucy grinned at her husband again. "As soon as you get some time, come on over to the ranch. I'm always there."

"Because she doesn't trust anyone but herself to take care of the horses," Reese said wryly.

"Wrong, I trust you." When he quirked an eyebrow at her, she added, *"Now."*

Their food arrived, and Reese and Lucy said their goodbyes. Once the waiter was gone, too, Caleb looked at Shelby. "See? No reason for you to think about leaving. Reese and Lucy's place is close to mine. So looks like you'll be busy for a while, yet."

"It does, doesn't it?" Satisfied, she turned to her meal and was unaware that Caleb watched her silently for a long minute, lost in his own thoughts.

Later that night, Caleb was restless. Maybe it was seeing Marta again. He hadn't seen her in more than six months and truth be told he hadn't given her another thought since the last time he'd walked out of her apartment. All they'd shared was sex. Great sex, but nothing more than that. So if he hadn't thought about her in all this time, why would seeing her today make him feel like he was about to jump out of his skin?

"Because it's not Marta," he muttered. "And it's not

seeing Reese and Lucy so damn happy and now pregnant on top of it."

No, it was the memory of holding Shelby. The feel
of her. The smell of her. The touch of her hand at his
waist and the feel of her head against his chest. They'd
left Houston soon after a late lunch and the minute
they got back to the ranch, Caleb had dived into work
to keep his body so busy his mind wouldn't have time
to dredge up images to torture him with.

That hadn't worked.

Hell, nothing had. He hadn't been able to stop thinking about Shelby all evening. Caleb had even skipped
dinner because he hadn't trusted himself to sit across
a table from her and not make a move. So now he was
restless *and* hungry.

He walked through the silent house without making
a sound. Caleb didn't bother to hit the light switches.
He could have found his way around blindfolded. The
kitchen was dark, as always, once Cam had cleared
up and gone home. There was just moonlight sliding
through the windows, casting a pale glow over everything. He noticed as he walked into the huge room that
Shelby had made some headway in the kitchen, too.

His mother had collected kitchen appliances. Antiques, new, didn't matter. She had teapots, kettles,
coffeepots, mixers and so many bowls she could have
opened her own pottery shop. His mom had been like
a magpie—if something shiny caught her eye, she had
wanted it.

But Caleb didn't want to think about his mother—or
Shelby. He just wanted to grab some cold fried chicken
and then try to get some sleep before morning.

He was halfway to the fridge when he heard a voice

from the eating nook by the bay window. "I think I should tell you, you are not alone."

"Shelby." Caleb stopped dead, glanced over his shoulder and spotted her in a slant of moonlight.

"Good guess," she said. Her head tipped to one side, spilling that beautiful hair of hers across one shoulder. "Got it in one."

"Why are you sitting here in the dark?" *Why are you in the kitchen*, he asked silently.

"The moonlight's pretty and light enough." She shrugged. "What're you doing sneaking around in the dark?"

"I don't sneak," he corrected and suddenly felt like an idiot for having done just that. What had it come to when he slipped through a quiet house in the dark to avoid seeing the woman driving him crazy? "Besides, this is my house and—" He sniffed the air. "Do you have the chicken?"

"Yes and it's great." She pushed a plate of chicken into the middle of the table. "Cam is a fantastic cook. Did you know she went to a culinary school in Park City, Utah, when she was a teenager? She told me stories about some of the chefs she met there and you wouldn't believe—"

"Stop." He held up one hand. "Just stop talking. I beg you. I came down here for some damn chicken before I sleep."

"No problem. Get a plate."

"Don't need a plate."

"Yeah, you do." She scooted off the bright blue bench seat and hurried past him to a cupboard.

He watched her go and swallowed the groan that rose up to choke him. She was wearing a tiny tank top and a pair of low-slung cotton shorts that just barely managed to cover her crotch. He couldn't tell what color they were. The moonlight disguised that. Could have been white or gray or yellow. And it didn't matter.

Her long legs looked silky and all too tempting. Her curly red hair fell loose around her shoulders, sliding back and forth with her every movement and he couldn't seem to look away.

"Here. Now sit down." She passed him again and he caught her scent. Unlike Marta's heavy floral perfume, Shelby smelled like summer. Fresh and clean and cool. She set the plate and a fork and napkin down opposite where she was seated. "I've got Cam's potato salad out, too. I wasn't hungry at dinner but a little while ago, I realized I could probably eat one of your cows, hooves and all, so…here we are."

"Yeah." He sat down and tried not to think of just how lovely she looked in moonlight. How close she was. All he had to do was stretch one arm across the table and he could take her hand, smooth his thumb across her palm, feel her pulse race.

She leaned forward and her thin tank top dipped slightly, allowing him an all too brief glimpse of her breasts. Somewhere there was a god of lust with a nasty sense of humor. He'd spent most of the afternoon and evening avoiding her and now she was here and he was more than tempted.

"Thanks again for taking me to Houston today."

Burying another groan, Caleb took a bite of chicken and scooped up some of Cam's famous potato salad. "Stop thanking me."

"I tried, but I can't seem to," Shelby said, taking a

sip from the water bottle in front of her. "So you'll just have to get used to it."

Caleb sighed, filled his plate and then stood to open the fridge and grab a bottle of water. In the slash of bright light that lit up the room, Shelby looked far more delicious than the chicken he'd come in here for. Her nipples were outlined against the thin fabric of her tank top and that wonderful hair of hers fell in tumbled curls across her shoulders. Her green eyes were clear and bright and locked on him.

He let the door swing shut, cutting off the light, slamming the room into darkness again.

"I was avoiding you tonight." His eyes adjusted quickly to the dim glow of the moonlight sliding through the window she sat beside.

"Yeah," she said softly. "I picked up on that when you didn't come in until after dark. Why do you think I'm here now?"

"You set a trap?"

"Oh, *trap* is a hard word."

Maybe, but he had the distinct impression it was accurate, too. "What was the plan?"

"Do I need one?"

No. All she had to do was sit there, staring at him, looking like a promise. Something stirred inside him, and Caleb did his best to smother it. Hell, he was the one who needed a damn plan.

She was talking again. Of course.

"I knew you had to get hungry at some point. We ate a long time ago."

"Oh, I am." He stared directly into her eyes so she could see he wasn't talking about the damn chicken now.

"Me, too," she whispered.

Everything in Caleb twisted into painful knots. "This is a bad idea."

"Oh, no doubt," she agreed, but she didn't look away.

Caleb had the opening there. The chance to back the hell off. This was the Godzilla of bad ideas. And that still wasn't enough to sway him from taking what he wanted.

"Damn it, Shelby," he ground out.

"Oh," she said softly, "you're talking too much."

He choked out a harsh laugh, took two long steps, pulled her to her feet and kissed her like he'd wanted to for days.

Since the moment she'd run into his arms while escaping her wedding.

Six

She felt even better against him *now*, Caleb thought.

Her arms snaked around his neck, she leaned into him and opened her mouth under his. Their tongues twisted and tangled together. Breath came fast and hard. Hearts pounded, blood boiled and need rose up, quickening with each passing second.

Caleb's hands moved up and down her back, tracing her spine with his fingertips. Then he swooped down again, his hands settled on her butt and squeezed, pressing her to his aching groin in a futile effort to ease the throbbing within. She sighed in response and that soft sound of surrender crashed down on him.

Caleb groaned, lifted her off her feet and spun her around until her back was against the wall. Breaking their kiss, he looked into her eyes and saw passion glittering in the moonlight.

"Don't stop," she said, her voice a whispered plea.

"Won't," he promised and slid one hand down the front of her shorts.

She gasped and tipped her head back against the wall as he touched her. Damp heat welcomed him and she hooked her legs around his hips, and arched into him. He stroked her center, driving them both a little crazy. She rocked her hips into his hand and let her breath pant from her lungs. When he pushed one finger, then two, deep inside her, she gasped and shuddered in his grasp.

"Caleb!" Her body trembled and her eyes closed briefly as she savored what he was doing to her.

He caressed her, inside and out, his thumb brushing over the heart of her, and as he watched her react, his body tightened to the point of agony. He hadn't wanted this to happen. Hadn't wanted to start something between them that would lead them both exactly nowhere. And now he couldn't imagine *not* touching her. She was driving him wild with desire. Had been from the moment he first saw her.

Caleb wanted her so much he could hardly breathe. He wanted—*needed*—to slide his body into hers, to feel her surround him and take him in. Darkness filled the room but between them there was light and heat and a bone-searing desire.

Touching her was filling him up and tearing a hole in him at the same time. It was good, but it wasn't enough. He needed more. Wanted more. She was a craving like nothing he'd ever known before and he poured his own desire into touching her more deeply, thoroughly, until her breath came short, fast. Until her body coiled in expectation. Until release slammed into her and she shook with the force of it. Until he held her in the darkness and felt her heart race against his.

At last, she took a long, deep breath, looked up into his eyes and grinned. "Wow."

Caleb stared at her for a second or two, then choked out a laugh. "You surprise me."

Tipping her head to one side, she asked, "Why? Did you expect regret? No. How could I be sorry *that* happened?"

He eased her onto her feet, letting her body slide against his, just because he was apparently a masochist and needed a bit more torture. Now that the initial frenzy of hunger had faded and he didn't have his hands full of her, Caleb could think clearly again. Beyond what he wanted to what he knew, so he took a long step backward and shook his head.

"This isn't going to happen."

"It already did," she said. "And at least from my point of view, it was really good."

He smiled briefly and wondered what it was about this woman that she could drive him nuts one second and make him laugh the next. She was honest and strong and funny and so damn hot, she was keeping him twisted into knots. Knots that couldn't be undone because there was nothing here for him. Nothing more than giving her a place to stay until she got her life back. Then it was done. He didn't need another woman in his life. Especially one who, like Meg, had made the choice to run from a situation rather than face it.

"Yeah, well," he muttered thickly, because each word cost him, "good time's over."

"What's going on, Caleb?" she asked, reaching out to him.

He grabbed her hand, squeezed it, then let her go. "Nothing, Shelby. That's the point."

Because he didn't trust himself to leave if he stayed even one more second, Caleb grabbed the damn plate of chicken and left her there in the dark.

Rose took extra care with her hair and makeup before her next meeting with Gus. Not for his benefit, of course. It was a small vanity to know that she'd kept her looks but for a few stubborn wrinkles she tried to ignore and the subtle gray streaks in her hair.

Her cream-colored slacks were matched with a butter-yellow shirt and a pair of light brown boots. The summer heat was at a blistering level, which made her grateful for the shade of the old oak she sat beneath. While she waited for Gus—who was late again—she checked her email. When she saw one from her grandson, Daniel, she frowned.

Gran,
Meeting a friend for dinner. Will be out late.
See you tomorrow,
Daniel

"A friend," she mused and tapped her well-manicured finger against the now darkened screen. She knew very well whom he was meeting. Alexis Slade. Did he think she was blind? Or too old to recognize the signs a man gave off when he'd found a woman he was interested in? She remembered all too well how Gus had once looked at *her*.

Her husband, Ed, never had, but then why would he? He'd been handpicked by her father to be her husband because Ed had been willing to take the Clayton surname and keep the family line going. Romance had had nothing to do with it.

Sliding her phone back into her purse, Rose looked up when she heard Gus approaching. He was still tall, built tough and strong, and just watching him walk stirred things inside her better left unstirred. Standing, she said, "You're late. Again."

"Good to see you, too, Rosie."

The familiar name took her breath away for a second. No one but Gus had ever called her *Rosie* and he hadn't done it in close to fifty years. His expression let her know that he was as surprised as she was that he'd said it now.

He scrubbed one hand across his jaw, cleared his throat and said, "This thing with Alexis and Daniel is getting serious. You've got to keep your boy away from my girl. Alex is telling me she's meeting her girlfriend for dinner tonight, but she's never bought a new dress to go out with her friends. It's *him* she's meeting."

"I know it," she said, "and I think I've come up with a solution."

"Glad to hear it." He braced his feet wide apart, crossed his arms over his chest and waited.

"A charity bachelor auction," Rose said. The idea had come to her while she was watching some silly TV reality show. "It's perfect. Daniel will enter and meet other women—hopefully finding one more suitable than your Alexis."

"Suitable? There's nothing wrong with my girl," he said in a near growl.

Rose waved one hand at him. "You know very well

what I mean. Alexis is a perfectly nice woman, but neither of us wants those two together. Do we?"

His jaw worked as if he were chewing on words he didn't like the taste of. "No. We don't."

"Well, then." Rose picked up her purse again and rummaged inside. Pulling out a piece of paper, she handed it to him. "I've jotted down a few ideas. I thought Alexis could be a part of this, as well. Meet some new eligible bachelors to distract her from Daniel. She wouldn't bid on him so publicly."

He scanned her list, nodding as he read. "It's not bad. If we make it a fund-raiser—say for pancreatic cancer—Alexis will jump on board."

Rose's heart sank a little. Gus's wife, Sarah, had died of the disease two years ago and she knew how hard her passing had hit both Gus and Alexis. Royal was a small town and people were always willing to talk about other people's business. So even though Rose and Gus hadn't spoken in decades, she had been able to keep up with what was happening in his life.

"That's a wonderful idea, Gus."

He looked at her and seemed to study her forever before he spoke again. "Sarah missed having you in her life, Rose."

"I missed her, too." They'd been inseparable once, when they were girls. But then life happened and things had gotten so twisted around.

His voice was gruff, accusatory when he said, "You didn't have to cut her off just because you didn't want me."

Old pain echoed inside Rose. She'd never told anyone why she'd acted as she had so long ago and it was too late now to dredge it all up again.

"You don't know what happened, Gus."

"Then tell me."

"What purpose would it serve now?" she asked, "After all these years?"

"Purpose? Truth is its own purpose."

"Truth isn't always kind."

"What the hell does *kind* have to do with anything?" Gus scowled at her and his tanned features twisted with it. "Damn it, Rose, you owe me the explanation I never got."

"We're here to talk about the kids."

"We're finally talking after too many damn years. So while we're at it, let's get to the bottom of all this." He tucked the paper into his shirt pocket, balled his fists on his hips and gave her a cool stare. "What the hell changed while I was off making enough money for us to get married? Why'd you cut me loose?"

It seemed they were going to do this, after all. And maybe he was right. Maybe he was owed that long-held explanation. "My father wanted me to marry Ed. To make sure that happened, he threatened me. Told me that he'd take away my mother's doctor. Her medicine, if I didn't break it off with you."

Gus snorted. "He wouldn't have done it."

"Yes, he would." Rose thought back to her life under Jedediah Clayton's thumb. Her father had ruled his slice of Texas through fear and intimidation and no one had been spared. Rose's mother had always been delicate and Jedediah used that to keep Rose in line.

"Papa didn't like you. Didn't like me wanting something of my own, so he stopped it." She swallowed hard as she met Gus's eyes. "He *made me* stop it."

"That's it?" Gus was astonished. And furious. "You sent me away because you were afraid of your father?"

"Not for myself," she argued. "If it was just me, I'd have defied him. But I couldn't risk my mother. I was a kid, Gus," she reminded him. "I had no power. I couldn't stand up to him."

Gus turned away, then spun back around to face her. "*We* could have, Rose."

"You weren't there," she said. "I had no way of contacting you. Finding you. I had to do what I did to save my mother."

"You didn't give me a chance. Didn't give *us* a chance."

She shook her head, unwilling to even consider the possibility now that she could have done something different all those years ago. "You didn't know him."

"Damn it, Rosie, you should have trusted *me*!"

His shout thundered in the air.

"It wasn't about *you*, Gus. It was about my mother. When you went away to make enough money for us to get married, I was alone with him. He was in charge and he never let me forget it." Damned if she'd apologize for doing what she had to, to protect her mother. "I kept hoping you'd come back, but you didn't. You were gone four years, Gus."

"For us, Rose."

"But in those years, my father ate away at my mother, at me, until there was nothing left. I was alone," she repeated for both their sakes. "I did what I had to."

Shaking his head, he looked at her. "You cut me off, fine. But you cut Sarah off, too."

Heart twisting, Rose said, "Sarah was my best friend.

Do you think I didn't miss her? Didn't *need* her, especially with you gone?"

"Then why?" he asked, voice tight and low.

"My father. He wouldn't allow it. Wouldn't allow me to have anything he didn't give me."

"I hope that old bastard's burning in hell," Gus muttered.

"You are not alone," she assured him.

Shaking his head, Gus asked, "Were you happy at least?"

She gave him a wry smile. For more than forty years, Rose had kept the secret of her hellish marriage. To outsiders, the Claytons were town royalty. Happy. Successful. But in reality, "Ed drank too much. When he did, he—"

"Did he hit you?"

Rose met his gaze and saw flashes of fire there. "Just once."

"Just *once*?" Gus's eyes nearly popped out of his head. "Damn it, Rose. Why the hell would you stay with him?"

"Where was I supposed to go?" she demanded. "He was drunk when he hit me and I hit him back. Let him know I wouldn't stand for that. You were already married. To Sarah. I'd lost my love and my best friend. I had no one else. I had my children. So I stayed. And I kept out of Ed's way."

"I can't believe what I'm hearing," Gus muttered and shot her another hard look.

"Oh, stop it, Gus. I'm not a battered woman. I'm not a victim."

"He hit you."

"Once."

"And that's okay?" His voice was thunderous again.

"Of course not." God, how had this gone so wrong? She hadn't meant to paint herself as a pitiable figure. "I survived my marriage. I kept my children safe. And now I've got Daniel and he is the light in my eye."

Gus's jaw worked furiously and Rose knew that he wanted to curse a blue streak. But she also knew he would never swear like he wanted to in front of a woman, so he was stuck.

"I'm not looking for sympathy," she said. "The past is past. Ed's gone now and I live my life the way I like it."

"You always did have spine," Gus mused. "It's why I always wondered why you didn't stand up to your daddy."

"For myself, I would have," Rose reiterated. "I couldn't risk my mother."

"Guess I understand that." He took off his hat and scrubbed his hand across his shaggy, silver hair. "But you should have told me. Told Sarah. You didn't have to cut yourself off from everydamnbody."

"Yes, I did." Rose smiled and shook her head sadly. "How could I watch you and Sarah being happy together when I—" She stopped, held up one hand and fought for control. Blast it, she hadn't meant to open up any of this mess and now that she had, she needed a way out.

Rose strove for dignity. Lifting her chin, she said simply, "I'm happy you and Sarah had so many good years together."

As if he understood that she had said all she was going to say about the past, Gus nodded. "We did. And now you and I are going to make sure our grandchildren have the futures they should have. Right?"

"Right." Grateful to be back on solid ground, Rose

took a seat on the bench and patted it. "Have a seat, Gus, and let's talk about the bachelor auction."

"A man auction," Gus said with a shake of his head. "Who would have thought it?"

"Earth to Shelby," Camilla said with a laugh.

"Huh? What?" Shelby gave herself a mental shake and looked at the other woman. "I'm sorry. Zoned out there for a second."

"Again," Cam pointed out.

Shelby sighed as she gave Caleb's housekeeper her full attention. Cam was short, curvy and had a long, blond braid that hung across one shoulder, and her blue eyes were shining with amusement.

"You're right." Returning to the task at hand, Shelby looked into the trunk of Caleb's big Suburban and let her gaze slide across all of the crystal packed in there carefully. "Now I'm back, though. This is everything?"

Cam nodded. "Everything we set aside for the first trip, anyway. Mrs. Mackenzie really did hold on to a lot of stuff."

"She did, but I've seen worse," Shelby told her.

"I'm glad I haven't." Cam shook her head. "And I can't even tell you how happy I am that you're clearing this stuff out. I know Caleb is, too."

"He hasn't said much one way or the other," Shelby said. Her gaze slid across the yard to the stable, then to the barn. There was no sign of Caleb, but that was hardly surprising. Since their little interlude in the kitchen two nights ago, he'd been darn near invisible.

"Well, take it from me, he's happy," Cam said. "Before you showed up the man couldn't even sit down in the great room. Now it's more like a home than a warehouse."

A home that Caleb was avoiding. Because of *her*. A spurt of irritation spiked inside her and Shelby let it fester and grow. She'd tried to be understanding. But honestly, the man was acting like she'd laid out an ambush for him and then thrown herself at him.

Well, okay, she had set him up, sitting in the dark, waiting for him. But what happened after that was on both of them. For heaven's sake, why was he acting as if they'd done something *wrong*? And why was he making her feel as though it was all her fault?

"Shelby?"

"I'm sorry, Cam." Shelby glanced at all of the crystal she was supposed to be taking into the Priceless antiques store, then looked at the woman beside her. "Can you do me a huge favor? Could you drive this stuff into town? I have to find Caleb."

Cam frowned a little, but nodded. "Sure. No problem. But you know Caleb's out on the range somewhere. You'll have to get a horse."

"I can ride," she said, with more certainty than she felt. Shelby hadn't ridden a horse in years. But it had to be like riding a bike, right? Some things you didn't forget.

"Okay, then. Ask my husband where Caleb went. He'll point you in the right direction."

An hour later, Shelby spotted Caleb in the distance. It shouldn't have taken so long, but since she hadn't ridden a horse in forever, Mike had insisted on giving her a mare with all the energy of a snail. But the sky was a blue so pure and deep, it almost hurt to look at it. The sun shone down like fire from heaven and the surrounding pastureland was varying shades of dusty green and brown. There were cattle grazing and she was glad to note they were on the other side of a fence that seemed to stretch on forever.

As Shelby rode closer, she enjoyed the look of pure surprise etched into Caleb's handsome features. She'd enjoy it a lot more if she wasn't already starting to ache all over.

"What the hell are you doing out here?"

"Well, that was charming."

"I'm not trying to be charming," he ground out, "I'm trying to *work*."

"Good to see you, too," Shelby said and took a good, long look at him. Caleb was tightening a strand of barbed wire around a fence post. He'd taken his shirt off and the sight of that tanned, muscular chest made Shelby's mouth go dry. If he weren't scowling at her, she'd have melted a little.

"How'd you find me? And since when do you ride horses?"

"Mike told me where you'd be and I took lessons for years as a kid." She looked down at him while her horse nuzzled his.

Still scowling, he bent his head to his work. "Fine. You found me. Go away."

Both eyebrows arched high on her forehead. "This must be that Southern hospitality I've heard so much about."

"Damn it, Shelby, I'm busy."

"Me, too. I'm supposed to be taking a load of your mother's crystal into town right now."

"Why aren't you, then?"

"Cam's taking it for me because I told her I had to talk to *you*. Who knew it would be this difficult?" She swung her leg over the horse's back and jumped down from the stirrups. Taking a step toward him, she stopped, said, "Ow," and rubbed her behind.

"Serves you right," he muttered. "Haven't ridden in years, then hop on a horse and ride for miles? Be lucky if you can walk tomorrow."

"If you'd quit avoiding me," she said, "I wouldn't have had to resort to this."

"I'm not avoiding you." He turned his back on her and her gaze instinctively dropped to his butt. Yeah, the view from this angle was pretty spectacular, too.

"Me being out here has nothing to do with you. I'm working," he reminded her.

"Right." She didn't believe it for a minute and was surprised that he thought she might. "And you don't go to the kitchen for food anymore, so what? You're dieting?"

He sent her a glare, tied off the wire and clipped the excess. Tucking that bit of wire into a worn, cowhide belt he wore draped around his hips, he yanked off his gloves, tipped his hat back and fired a long, hard look at her. "What do you want? An apology? Fine. I'm sorry."

"You never listen, do you? I already told you I don't regret what happened."

He snorted. "You should."

"Why?"

He ignored her, tucking his work gloves into the saddlebags. Shelby laid one hand on his forearm and demanded again, "Why?"

Caleb looked from her hand to her eyes. "Because,

damn it," he ground out, "there's nothing here for you, Shelby. Not with me."

Her hand dropped away. "I never asked you for anything."

"Not yet."

She swayed back a little, almost as if his words had delivered a physical shot. "Are you under the impression I'm trying to trick you into a relationship or something?"

"You said yourself you waited in the dark for me the other night."

"Yes, because I was attracted to you," she snapped. "Though right now I don't remember why."

He took off the belt, hooked it on his saddle horn, then turned back around to face her. His jaw was tight, mouth grim and those icy eyes of his looked steely and dangerous. "I gave you a place to stay…"

"And I'm grateful—"

"Not the point." He held up one hand for quiet. "I don't go around using women just because they're handy."

Shelby just stared at him. "I don't let myself be used, either, so we're on the same page there."

"All I'm saying is that you're not the one-night kind of woman and that's all I've got to offer you—" He broke off, turned to snatch his shirt out of a saddlebag and then shrugged into it, leaving it unbuttoned. "So I'm staying clear of you."

"I don't know what to feel here," Shelby admitted, watching him, sorry to see him cover most of that really great chest. "Should I be flattered you think I'm worth more than one night? Or offended that you think I'm waiting for you to get down on one knee and promise me forever?"

"I didn't say—"

"No, you already said what you had to," Shelby said, and this time held up *her* hand for quiet. His mouth quirked at the gesture. "Now it's my turn. I'm grateful that you gave me a place to stay—but I don't need you to take care of me. To protect me. I'm a big girl—"

"I noticed."

Her mouth twitched briefly. "We're two adults, Caleb. If we want to be together, why shouldn't we? I don't expect anything from you—no wait. That's wrong. I do have one expectation."

"Yeah?" Wary now, he watched her.

Irritated, she said, "Oh, for heaven's sake. You really don't listen at all, do you? Stop getting that trapped look in your eyes."

He frowned at her, folded his arms across his chest and huffed out a breath. "Fine. What's your expectation?"

"That you'll stop avoiding me." She moved in on him, closing the distance between them. A soft, hot wind blew across the land, lifting her hair and blowing the edges of Caleb's shirt back. "That you'll kiss me again. Often."

As if thinking about what she'd said, he took a deep breath and released it slowly as he shifted his gaze to the wide pasture stretching out behind her. Several long seconds passed before he met her gaze again and when he did, Shelby saw storm clouds in his eyes.

"Damn it, woman." He set his hands at her hips and Shelby sighed as the accompanying rush of heat swept through her. "You should be careful what you wish for."

"I'm not wishing, Caleb. I'm *saying*." She reached

up and tugged the brim of his hat lower over his eyes. Smiling at him, she said, "Stop pretending there's nothing between us."

"And if I do?" His voice was a low growl that hummed across her skin. His hands at her hips tightened, and Shelby sighed a little.

"If you do, then we're good." She stepped out of his grasp, took a step toward her horse and said, "And now that we both know where we stand, I'll go back to the house."

In a blink, he grabbed her hand, tugged her to him and then fisted one hand in her hair. Pulling her head back, he kissed her like a dying man looking for salvation. His tongue demanded, his breath pumped into her and when he finally let her go, Shelby's knees wobbled.

Looking deeply into her eyes, he said softly, "*Now* we're good."

Seven

When Caleb rode back into the ranch yard a couple hours later, his mind was on Shelby. As it had been since she'd left him and ridden back to the house. He'd thought it through and come to the conclusion that she was right. They were adults. They clearly wanted each other. So what the hell was he waiting for? Kissing her had fed the fires inside until it felt as if the Texas summer sun couldn't even compete with what was happening within.

The yard was busy. A couple of the men working with horses in the corral, two more putting a fresh coat of white paint on the stable fence. It was hot and miserable and Caleb wasn't thinking about work. All he wanted now was to find Shelby and ease the ache that had been torturing him for days.

Then he noticed the shining silver Porsche parked near the front door. Scowling at the thought of unexpected company, Caleb swung down from his horse, tossed the reins to Mike and jerked his head at the car. "Who's here?"

Mike frowned. "Jared Goodman."

"Hell." Caleb swiped one hand across his face and gritted his teeth. He supposed it made sense that Jared would show up eventually. But why *now*? "What did Shelby say?"

Mike shrugged. "When I saw him drive up, I went to the house, offered to stay with her while Jared was here but she insisted she was okay."

That sounded like her. Stubborn and strong and independent as hell. "Is Cam in there?"

"Nope." Mike shook his head and stared at the house as if he could see through the walls to what was happening inside. "She went into town a couple hours ago. Not back yet."

So Shelby was alone. With a man who had to be furious at the humiliation she'd served him. Caleb remembered all too well how he'd felt when Meg had dumped him in favor of his brother. It hadn't been pretty. The thought of Shelby facing Jared down alone was something he didn't care for. Though why it bothered him, he wasn't willing to explore. "I'll see about it."

Caleb trotted across the ranch yard, opened the front door and the first thing he heard was Shelby's voice. She was talking fast. Not a surprise.

"I'm really sorry, Jared, but I did the right thing. You'll see that, eventually."

"Right." Jared's voice came across in a sneer. "I'm sure I'll be real happy that my bride ran out on me in front of the whole damn town."

They were in the great room and Caleb moved quietly across the hall, so he could see what was going on. If she was handling things all right, he could always slip out again. She wouldn't even have to know that he'd checked in on her.

But he was distracted almost instantly. His first impression was, he hardly recognized the damn place. Since Shelby had been at the house, he'd been coming and going through the doors in his wing. Hell, he'd been using those doors since his mother started her "collection." Caleb hadn't seen the great room since Shelby went to work on it.

And in a matter of just a few days, she'd cleared the place of all the extra cabinets and dressers and the mountain of crystal and glassware. This was a room people could sit in. There were couches and chairs he barely remembered and a couple of tables that belonged there, but the room was once again a huge space with a wide, unobstructed view of the ranch yard. Of course, at the moment, the custom wooden shutters were closed over the glass, keeping this little scene private.

But his interest in the room faded as he focused on the man standing way too close to Shelby. Jared Goodman, like his father, stood a few inches shorter than Caleb. His black hair was slicked back and his gray suit looked out of place on a ranch. His features were twisted with anger and his eyes flashed sparks of heat as he loomed over Shelby.

Beyond the slash of fury that surprised the hell out of him, Caleb felt a quick jolt of admiration to see Shelby holding her own. She faced the man down and didn't look the least bit worried.

"I've heard the stories your mother's put out," Shelby

said calmly. "The word is that you're the one who called things off."

"But *we* know the truth, don't we, Shelby?" His voice was low and hard.

Impatient, she huffed out a breath. "Jared, it's over. We never should have tried this and you know that, too. I let myself believe that I was in love, but the truth is, I wasn't. I was just really flattered at how you swept me off my feet and that's not enough to build anything on, Jared—and you know it, too." She sighed a little, then added, "Honestly, you wouldn't be happy with me anyway. I talk too much and I'm a little bossy and I like to organize things all the time and you hate that. I mean, look at your office, it's just a mess, with files everywhere. We would never work out."

Jared tried to get a word in and failed. Caleb almost felt sorry for him.

"It's just that I'm sure you'll find the right person for you, but that's not me and it won't change, so we should just shake hands and part friends. I can do that, Jared," she said, "can you?"

"Friends?"

She gave him a sympathetic smile that was completely wasted on him. "Oh, Jared. This was never going to work. Really, it never should have *started*. So I'm sorry for that. But I'm not sorry for leaving."

"We're not friends," Jared snapped when Shelby finally wound down. He moved in closer and Caleb didn't like the look on the man's face. "You don't get to just walk away from me."

Okay, that was enough.

"She already did." Both people turned to look at him

as Caleb walked across the room to stand beside Shelby. "You should go, Jared."

Shelby was clearly startled to see him, but Jared's features went tight and even harder.

"What the hell do you have to say about any of this, Mackenzie?"

"Caleb—" Shelby started talking, but Caleb cut her off.

He kept his gaze fixed on Goodman. "For one thing, this is my house. My land. You've got no business here, Goodman, and no right to stand here trying to intimidate Shelby. You're not welcome and it's time for you to go."

"I'll go when I'm ready," Jared said. "You don't worry me, Mackenzie."

"I should, though." Caleb wrapped one arm around Shelby's shoulders and pulled her in to his side. "I work hard for a living, Goodman. You push papers. So don't try to throw your weight around in my place."

Jared's gaze fixed on the way Caleb was holding her.

"That's right. Shelby's with me, now, Jared." She stiffened against him and Caleb hoped to hell that she for once, didn't start talking. "She ended your relationship when she ran out on the wedding. So I don't want to see you back here again. You had some things to say and you said them. So now you can go."

"That's why you walked out?" Jared demanded hotly, ignoring Caleb to focus on Shelby. "You expect me to believe you left me for *him*?"

"You can believe whatever you want," Caleb said before Shelby could speak.

"This is ridiculous."

Caleb dismissed him, bent to Shelby and gave her

a fast, hard kiss to prove to Jared that he was telling the truth. And with the taste of her in his mouth, he turned to glare at the other man. "Now get out before I toss you out."

Jared looked at Shelby. "You bitch."

Caleb took a step forward and was pleased to see Jared skitter backward. "That's it. Go."

He did, storming across the room and out the door, slamming it behind him just to continue the child-having-a-tantrum attitude. Before the echo of that loud slam had faded, Shelby pushed away from Caleb and stared up at him.

"Why did you do that?" She lifted both hands to her temples and squeezed. "It just makes everything harder. I was handling him. I didn't need help."

Caleb remembered the look on Jared's face as he towered over Shelby and he wasn't so sure about that. Even the most timid dog finally bit if it was pushed too far.

"Not how it looked to me," Caleb said, gazing down into worried green eyes. "Jared was just getting madder by the second and with a man like him, you can't trust his reactions."

"He wouldn't have hurt me!" She seemed astonished at the thought.

"He won't now, anyway," Caleb agreed.

Frowning, Shelby seemed to think about that for a second or two. Then something else occurred to her. "The Goodmans still have my clothes. My money. Do you think he's going to be helpful now?" Letting her hands drop, she sighed. "Now he thinks we're a couple and that's just going to make this an even bigger mess."

"Maybe." Caleb pulled his hat off and tossed it onto the nearest table. He hadn't really been thinking about what Jared might believe or what he might do down the road. Hadn't been thinking much at all. It was pure instinct that had driven him across the room to stand between Shelby and potential danger.

He'd acted on impulse and Caleb couldn't even say he was sorry about it. He dropped both hands on her shoulders and held on tight. "I don't give a damn what he thinks. No one comes into my house and bullies you. Nobody."

She slumped a little and gave him a smile that was part pleased and part impatience. "That's really sweet, but didn't I tell you I don't need you to protect me?"

"Yeah, but turns out, *I* needed to protect you."

"Oh, Caleb. You realize this is only going to make the Goodmans even more furious with me." She chewed at her bottom lip. "Jared will tell his parents what you said and his mother will be spreading even more gossip. And now, you've told her she was right all along and that I'm with you."

"She already thought it. Remember?"

"Now she has your word on it. And then you just had to kiss me in front of Jared."

"He's not real bright," Caleb mused. "Thought he could use a visual aid."

"It's not funny, Caleb," she said, though her mouth curved briefly. Shaking her head, she said, "They'll never give me back my things now. And Jared's still got my money. I can't find a place to live or start a business or even move back to Chicago without that money."

Caleb frowned when she mentioned moving away. He hadn't really thought about it, but there was nothing holding her in Royal—or Texas, for that matter. She'd come to get married and now that she wasn't…well, hell.

"That what you're planning?" he asked. "To move back to Chicago?"

She looked up at him. "Honestly, I haven't thought that far ahead yet. What's the point? I can't plan anything until I have access to my money."

Not an answer, but it wasn't important, was it? Hadn't he been trying to avoid her for days? So why should he care if she moved out of state? Wouldn't that be the perfect ending to this situation? Shaking his head, he shoved those thoughts aside and got back to the matter at hand.

"The bank emailed you the receipt for the sale of your house, for the deposit," Caleb reminded her. "If Nate doesn't get the money for you, the judge will have the Goodmans turn it over."

She blew out a breath and nodded. "That's true. I have proof that the money is mine. They can't keep it. And I know I shouldn't get so worked up over Jared, but this is all my fault. I never should have said yes when he proposed but it seemed right at the time, you know?"

She wasn't looking for a conversation, Caleb knew. This was another rant and damned if he wasn't starting to enjoy them.

"I never meant to pull you into the middle of all this, Caleb," she said, pushing one hand through her hair. "You were just being nice and I told you I didn't need to be defended, but it was really sexy when you came in and kissed me and told Jared to get out, and it shouldn't have been, but I can't help how I feel about it, can I?

"I mean, it's so old-world cowboy movie for you to come striding in with your hat and your stoic expression and be all—" she scrunched up her face and deepened her voice "—'That's my woman, so back off,' and for some reason, it made my stomach do a dip and spin that took my breath away—"

That's my woman. He hadn't meant it like that. Not really. He was pretty sure. But Caleb could admit that seeing Jared looming over Shelby, bullying her just by being bigger and taller than her had really pissed him off, so that all he could think to do was stand in front of her. To get rid of Jared so her face wouldn't look so damn pale.

And now, all he wanted was for her to quiet down and the best way to do that, he'd already discovered, was...

He kissed her.

Like he had out on the range, one hand in her dark auburn curls, holding her head still so he could take his time and indulge in the taste of her. And in less than a second, she was kissing him back, hooking one leg around his, snaking her arms around his waist and holding on. His tongue caressed hers. He took her breath as his and gave her back his own. Then held her so tightly, he could feel the soft, full mounds of her breasts against his chest. Her hips ground into his, spiking the ache in his groin to epic proportions. He'd never known the kind of want she inspired in him. Never experienced the kind of desperation pushing at him.

He lifted his head, looked down into those grass-green eyes of hers and saw them shining with the same kind of pulsing desire hammering at him. "I want you, Shelby. Right the hell now."

"What took you so long?" She grinned, then kissed him, opening her mouth to him, tasting him as he had her. Her hands went to his belt. He felt her unhook the damn thing and undo the top button of his jeans. Then she tugged the hem of his shirt free and slid her hands up beneath the fabric to stroke her palms across his chest.

He sucked in a gulp of air, lifted his head and smiled. "Glad you cleared out this room so nicely. Because that couch is a hell of a lot handier than a bedroom."

"Yes," she said on a breathy sigh and flicked her thumbs across his flat nipples.

He gritted his teeth and felt every drop of blood in his body rush to his groin. He was hard and aching and if he didn't have her in the next few minutes, Caleb was sure he'd die.

In two steps they were at the couch and he tipped her back onto it in one smooth motion. She landed with a thump and laughed up at him.

Her eyes were shining, her delectable mouth curved in a smile that promised all sorts of wicked things. When she tore off her tank top to reveal a skimpy piece of sky blue lace covering her breasts, he couldn't look away. Then she unhooked the front of the bra and let the delicate cups slide away, baring her breasts to him. In the cool, air-conditioned room, her dark pink nipples peaked instantly and Caleb didn't waste a second. He came down on top of her and took first one of those nipples, then the other, into his mouth. His lips, tongue and teeth tormented her while she writhed and panted beneath him.

She tugged at his shirt so furiously that he finally paused long enough in his enjoyment of her body to rise up and let her pull the shirt off. Then her hands were on him. Small, smooth, strong. She stroked, caressed and scored his skin with her short nails while he again suckled at her breasts.

"God you smell good," he whispered, lingering to give one nipple another licking kiss.

She shivered. "So do you."

Caleb laughed. "No I don't." He half pushed up from her. "Just wait. Give me five minutes in a shower and I'll be back—"

"No, you're not going anywhere," she said, shaking her head against the brown leather couch. She licked her lips, let her fingers trail down his chest, across his flat abdomen to the button fly of his jeans.

Caleb went perfectly still. He felt every skimming touch of her hands as she worked the buttons free, one by one. And with each inch of freedom gathered, his dick hardened further. Finally, she reached down and curled her small, strong hand around him and squeezed, while stroking up and down his length.

Caleb dropped his forehead to hers and took deep, deliberate breaths. If he didn't maintain control, he'd explode before he'd done what he'd been dreaming of doing to her. Reaching down, he grabbed her hand and held it pinned to the couch above her head.

"Don't. You'll push me over the edge and I want to stay there for a while."

His free hand dropped to the waistband of the knee-length white shorts she wore and quickly undid the snap and zipper. One glance told him her skimpy panties matched the blue lace bra and everything inside him twisted in response. One time, he wanted to see her dressed only in those wisps of lace. But now, he wanted her in *nothing*.

He slid down the length of her body, trailing kisses and long, slow licks as he went. She shivered again and he loved it. His hands tugged her shorts and panties free and when she was naked, he took a long moment to simply enjoy the view.

"Slide that bra all the way off," he ordered.

She ran her tongue slowly across her bottom lip, then lifted off the couch high enough to pull the bra off and drop it to the floor. When she stretched out on the couch again, she crooked a finger.

"You're wearing too many clothes."

"Yeah, I am." He kept his gaze fixed with hers while he quickly stripped, so he saw the flash of pleasure dart across her eyes when she saw him, long and hard and ready.

Her hips rose off the couch in eager anticipation. She planted her feet, parted her legs more widely and whispered, "Be inside me, Caleb."

Four little words that tore him to pieces. There was simply nothing he wanted more. But first… He took hold of her thighs, held them wide and looked at the core of her, hot and pink and wet. She was as ready as he was and that pushed him over that dangerous edge he'd been clinging to.

He bent his head to her, covering her center with his mouth, tasting her, licking at her, nibbling until she was whimpering, rocking her hips and softly begging him for what he wouldn't give her. Not yet.

Again and again, he teased her, tormented her, relishing every sigh and groan she made. She reached down and threaded her fingers through his hair as she cried his name brokenly.

He rode the power of her passion until he was nearly blind with the need choking him and only then did Caleb rise up, cover her body with his and slide into her heat.

He pushed deep and she wrapped her legs around his hips, giving him a better angle, allowing her to take all of him in. Locked together, they stared into each other's eyes as he moved inside her. He watched her eyes flash. Watched her lips part on a sigh that welled up from deep within her.

Caleb pushed deeper, higher, groaning as he filled her, as she surrounded him with a kind of heat that burst into an inferno within. Friction bristled between them as he set a rhythm that she raced to match. She was with him, every step of the way and he'd never known anything like this before. There was a connection here, linking them in ways that were more than physical. Everything she felt was stamped on her features. Every touch she bestowed on him left streaks of flame burning down into his bones. His blood.

Again and again, he moved, claiming her, taking them both well past that slippery edge until they were left, staggering wildly, fighting for balance, for release.

"Come now," he ordered, voice thick, strained with the effort to hold himself back when all he wanted to do was empty himself inside her.

She shook her head, gasping, panting. "We go together. Both of us."

Reaching down, she cupped him and rubbed, stroked him until he was beyond pleasure, beyond the boundaries of everything that had come before. And so he slid one hand between their bodies and stroked her core as he continued to pump into her.

And finally, together, they jumped off the edge and fell crashing into lights brighter than he'd ever seen before.

* * *

When her heart stopped racing, Shelby took a deep breath and closed her eyes in complete satisfaction. Her body was still buzzing, the echoes of a world-class orgasm still shuddering inside her. Sex had never been like that before. Until this moment, she'd always thought of it as a pleasant enough time that ended with a delicious little pop of release.

Caleb Mackenzie had changed all of that.

He knew things that all men should know. His hands were magic and his mouth should be bronzed. In fact, Shelby felt a bit sorry for every woman who had never been with him. While at the same time, she wanted to keep him all for herself and never let another woman near him.

A frown settled between her brows. Where had that thought come from? Caleb wasn't hers. There was nothing between them but convenience and blistering sex.

Well. That was nearly enough to take the shine off her feelings.

With his big, strong body pressing into hers, Shelby felt a stirring of a warmth that was slower and steadier than the heat she had just survived. That realization should have worried her. Instead, she took a second to revel in it. To enjoy this one perfect moment.

Then Caleb lifted his head, looked down at her and solemnly said, "This is a really bad time to be asking, but—are you on the Pill?"

There went the rest of the shine.

"Yes," she said and saw relief flicker in his eyes. "I've been on the Pill for a few years now so—" She broke off and thought about that for a second.

"What?" Caleb watched her warily. "What is it?"

"Probably nothing," Shelby assured him, though she wasn't as confident in that as she was trying to sound. Forcing a smile, she added, "I'm sure it's fine…"

"But?" he asked.

"*But*, remember I didn't have my purse for three days…"

"Yeah?" One word drawn out into five or six syllables.

"Well, my pills were in my purse, so…"

"So you didn't take any for a couple of days."

"No." He was literally right on top of her and she still felt him take a mental step backward. "I'm sure it's fine, though. I took the Pill yesterday and today and I'm sure I've got all kinds of those wonderful little hormones all stored up in my system."

"Uh-huh." Caleb pulled away, sat up and grabbed his jeans off the floor. "Damn it."

"No reason to panic," she said.

"Is that right?" He snorted a laugh and shook his head as he stood up to yank his jeans on.

It was a shame, she thought idly, to cover up that really amazing body.

"I don't know what I was thinking," Caleb said tightly, more to himself than to her. Then he looked at her. "I have *never* failed to use a damn condom."

"Until today." She shrugged, reached down for her blue bra and pulled it on.

"Yeah." He pushed one hand through his hair in sheer frustration. "Until today. Until *you*."

Shelby smiled. "The words sound like a compliment. The tone really doesn't."

"I should apologize, I guess, and if I can find a way to say it and sound like I mean it, I will."

Well, clearly their postcoital conversation was coming to an end with a whimper. Reaching down for her shirt, Shelby tugged it on, then grabbed her panties. Standing up, she wriggled into them and enjoyed the flash of interest in Caleb's eyes.

"No apology necessary," she said and stepped into her white shorts. Once they were snapped and zipped, she tossed her hair out of her eyes and said, "I didn't think of it, either. All I could think about was you. Having you inside me."

His eyes burned like a fire in ice. "Hell, that's all I can think of right now."

She gave him a slow smile and felt her body stirring. "Me, too. And I'm not going to regret that, no matter what else happens. Honestly, Caleb, I'm sure it's fine."

"Yeah." He sent her another long look. "You be sure and tell me if it's not."

"I will. But I'm not worried." Not quite true, so she added, "Well, maybe a little."

Grabbing his shirt off the floor, he tugged it on. "Not much slows you down, does it?"

"Well, what would be the point of being all…" She mocked tearing her hair out, throwing her head back to shriek, then looked at him and grinned. "Would it help to gnash my teeth and howl at the moon?"

His lips twitched and her heart gave a hard jolt.

Moving in closer to him, Shelby laid both hands on his chest and relished the heat when his hands cupped her shoulders. "My grandmother was Irish," she said softly, staring up into those beautiful eyes of his. "She always told me, 'If you worry, you die. If you don't worry, you die. So why worry?'"

Caleb just stared at her and, slowly, another smile

curved his mouth. "You always throw me for a loop, Shelby. Never sure just what you're going to say next."

"Well, then," she said, sliding her arms around his waist, "brace yourself. What do you say we both go and take a shower?"

He cupped her face between his palms, bent his head and kissed her softly, gently. Everything inside Shelby fluttered back into life again and now that she knew just what he was capable of, she trembled with it.

"I think," he said, "that's a great idea. Plus, there're condoms in the bathroom."

She looked up at him and grinned. "How many?"

"Let's find out." Caleb picked her up and tossed her over his shoulder. Shelby's laughter trailed behind them.

Eight

Mitch and Meg returned home the following morning and everything between Shelby and Caleb changed
in a blink of time.

In the rush and noise of the family arriving, and the
kids shrieking with joy to be home again, Shelby felt
Caleb pull away from her. He distanced himself so eas-
ily it was almost scary to watch. It was as if, for him,
the night they'd just shared had never happened.

Only that morning, she and Caleb had been wrapped
together in his bed, after a long night of incredible sex
and putting quite a dent in Caleb's condom supply.
They'd laughed and kissed and had a picnic in that bed
in the middle of the night and yet, the minute Mitch
and Meg had arrived, Caleb had shut down. He'd become cold. Distant.

With his family around, he was a different man.

Except with the twins, she reminded herself. The two children had thrown themselves at Caleb and he'd held nothing back with them, smiling, laughing, swinging them around.

It was when he faced Mitch and Meg and Shelby that his features turned to stone. He'd introduced her to them and briefly explained why she was there, but beyond that, he'd hardly spoken to her since his family arrived. She had to wonder why. Was it her? Was he pulling back to remind her that there was nothing but sex between them? Was he making sure his family understood that Shelby was only there temporarily?

And if he was trying to shut her out, why was he being so cold to his brother and sister-in-law, too?

To be fair, though, she had to admit that Meg and Mitch weren't exactly being warm and friendly toward Caleb, either. Families were complicated, she knew that, but there was more here than simple sibling issues. And she really wished she knew what exactly it was bubbling beneath the surface of the Mackenzie family. Maybe then she could find a way to reach Caleb.

She probably should have gone into the house and busied herself with the organizational job that wasn't finished yet. But for two hours, she sat on the porch instead, watching the family she didn't belong to. It was fascinating to watch the play of relationships and as she studied them all from the shade of the front porch, she tried to spot signs that might explain what was going on.

Mitch Mackenzie was a younger, shorter version of Caleb, but to her mind, Caleb was much better looking and she couldn't help but notice that the brothers were *cautious* around each other. They kept a safe distance between them as they stood at the corral watching a few of the men work the horses. If body language could actually speak, theirs would be shouting. The two men couldn't have been more ill at ease with each other.

Meg Mackenzie was tiny, just five feet or so, with short blond hair and big blue eyes. Her husband appeared to adore her, but Caleb barely acknowledged her existence. Caleb treated her with a cool detachment, hardly glancing her way. And Shelby wondered again just what was happening here. The Mackenzie family was simmering with tension.

Except when it came to the twins. At three years old, they looked like miniature Mackenzies. Jack and Julie were loud, adorable and seemed to have an infinite amount of energy. For a couple of hours, it was crazy while the kids ran around and Caleb and Mitch talked business. Meg was in and out of their house across the yard, settling in.

Shelby tried to stay out of the way because she could see there was friction between Caleb and his brother—not to mention Meg. She didn't want to add to the problems, so she kept to herself in a rocking chair on the porch.

She'd brought out a pitcher of iced tea, four glasses and a plate of homemade cookies. But so far, she was snacking all by herself. Still, she was in the shade and had a bird's-eye view of the Mackenzie family. But for the first time since coming to the ranch, she felt exactly what she was—an outsider.

With her gaze locked on Caleb, Shelby wished she could see what he was thinking. Feeling.

"Sometimes," she murmured, "stoic is just annoying."

Still, she couldn't look away from him. He and his

brother both stood, one booted foot on the bottom rung of the corral fence, their arms resting on the top rung. Did they even realize how alike they were? Or was that lost in whatever it was that was keeping them divided? She'd like to talk to Caleb, see what was driving the coolness that had dropped onto him like a shroud. But that wouldn't happen until he stopped shutting her out.

She took a sip of her tea then set her glass down on the table beside her. A hot wind bustled across the ranch, lifting her hair from the back of her neck and stirring the dust in the yard into a mini cyclone that dissipated as quickly as it rose up. The steady, pounding clop from the horses running in circles around the corral was like the heartbeat of the ranch. Shelby took a deep breath and let it slide from her lungs again.

Strange how much she'd come to love this place. The wide sky, the openness of the land, the horses... Caleb. And now she was forced to acknowledge that as much as she liked being there, she didn't *belong*. That admission hurt more than she would have expected and she wondered when this place, and this man, had become more than a port in the storm.

Then the twins spotted her and bulleted across the yard, headed right for her. Shelby smiled, watching their shining faces and those eyes, as bright a blue as the sky.

The little girl beat her brother by a couple of steps, climbed up onto Shelby's lap and grinned. Her soft brown hair was pulled into two impossibly short pigtails and she had a dimple in her right cheek. "Daddy says you live here. You do? Can I have a cookie?"

Hmm. Problem. How did she give them cookies without asking their mother first? Then Jack scrambled over, shouted "I like cookies!" and grabbed one, stuffing half of it into his mouth.

Not to be outdone, Julie squirmed on Shelby's lap until she could grab one, too. With crumbs on her cheek, Julie said, "Uncle Caleb lives here."

"Yes, he does."

"You like Uncle Caleb?" Jack demanded.

Danger zone, she thought and then dismissed it. The children were too young to read anything into her answers, so she kept it simple. "Yes, I do. Do you?"

"Uh-huh," Jack said. "He's funny."

"Uncle Caleb is crabby sometimes," Julie told her thoughtfully. "Can you make him not crabby?"

Out of the mouths of babes. Laughing, Shelby dusted the crumbs off the girl's face. "Well, I don't know, but I can try."

"I ride horsies," Jack announced.

"Ponies," Julie corrected, with a sisterly sneer.

"He's a *big* pony," her brother argued back.

"Okay, you two, take a hike."

Shelby hadn't even seen their mother arriving; she'd been too busy fielding questions and being entertained. Now Meg climbed the steps, sat down in the chair beside Shelby and sent both kids off with a cheerful, "Go bug your daddy for a while."

Both of them took off at a dead run toward the spot where Mitch and Caleb still stood side by side, yet separate, at the corral fence. Little Jack's small cowboy hat flew off and he circled back to snatch it out of the dirt. When Julie came up on her father, he swung her up to his shoulders. Then Caleb did the same for Jack when the boy tugged at his jeans.

The summer sun was blazing out of a bright blue sky

with only a few meager white clouds to mar the per-
fection of it. Shelby watched Caleb with the kids and
everything inside her melted.

"Sorry," Meg said, "the kids are so glad to be out
of the car, they're a little more excitable than usual."

"Oh, they're wonderful. And adorable, too."

"Well, you do know how to make points with moth-
ers," Meg said with a grin.

"I wasn't—" Shelby stopped herself and smiled.
"Sorry about the cookies. I should have asked you, but
they just—"

"Swarmed you?" Meg nodded in understanding.
"They double-team you and you don't stand a chance.
Trust me. I know."

"They're so cute."

"And busy." She patted her flat belly. "Hopefully this
next one will be a single."

"You're pregnant?" Her voice sounded a little wistful even to herself. "Congratulations."

"Thanks." Meg tipped her head to one side and studied Shelby for a couple of seconds. "You're staring."

Shelby jumped, startled away from looking at Caleb.
"Yeah. I guess I was."

Meg mused, "Handsome, aren't they?"

"Hard to argue with that."

"Of course," Meg said, "I'm partial to Mitch, but Caleb's not bad…" She slid a glance at Shelby and seemed
to like what she saw because her smile widened. Then
she poured a glass of tea, took a long drink and went
on to say, "Bless you for this. Honestly, visiting my
folks in Oregon, I forgot just how hot it was going to
be when we got home."

"It really is awful, isn't it?"

"Summer in Texas," Meg said on a sigh, "the devil's vacation spot. And, now that we've talked about the weather, why don't you tell me how you're doing after escaping your wedding and all?"

She blinked and swallowed hard. Just how much did Meg know? "What?"

"I heard about what happened."

"Caleb told you?"

"Oh, no." Meg shrugged and waved one hand at her. "You must have heard about the gossip chain in Royal."

"Yes, but you weren't here."

"Doesn't seem to matter," the other woman said and grabbed a cookie. "I love chocolate chip. Anyway, I called my friend Amanda—the sheriff's wife—to tell her she wasn't the only one pregnant, and she told me what happened at the wedding."

"Oh, God." Shelby covered her eyes with one hand as if she could simply hide from everyone with that one gesture. "This is so embarrassing."

Meg reached out and patted her hand. "Believe me when I say you don't have to be embarrassed."

"Well, I am," Shelby muttered, smoothing her palms across her khaki shorts.

"Why? Because you were strong enough to walk out of a marriage you knew would be a disaster?" Meg shook her head firmly. "As hard as it was, it was the right thing to do. Jared Goodman? No."

"That's embarrassing, too." Shelby looked at the woman next to her. It seemed weird to be talking about such private things with someone she'd only just met, but Meg had an open, friendly air that was hard to resist. "Why I didn't see what clearly everyone in Royal already knew."

Meg sighed and turned her gaze back to her husband and his brother. "I don't know. Sometimes I think we're deliberately blind to things we'd rather not admit."

Shelby wondered what Meg was thinking, but then, all of the Mackenzies seemed to have secrets and no outsider would breach the walls containing them.

Several hours later, Caleb told himself that this was the first time in memory he'd been glad to have a TCC meeting to attend. But he'd never needed to get away from the ranch more than he had today. With Mitch and Meg and Shelby all there, he felt like he had one foot caught in a damn bear trap.

He was glad his brother was back home, if only to share the burden of running the ranch. But things had been strained between them since Meg had walked out on Caleb to marry Mitch. He'd tried to get past it, but damn it, he was faced with the reality of what had happened every day.

It wasn't that he was still in love with Meg. Hell, that had faded faster than he'd thought possible and maybe every now and then he'd admitted to himself that it was possible his ex-fiancée had done the right thing— though she'd gone about it the wrong way.

Then there was Shelby. He'd gotten too close to her last night. Sex was one thing, but laughing and talking during and after that sex was another. Sure, being with her had been spectacular, better than anything he'd ever known before. But it wasn't the great sex that worried him.

It was sleeping with her in his bed. Waking up with her legs tangled with his. Staring down at her, waiting for her to open those beautiful green eyes and smile up at him.

Came too damn close to caring and he wasn't going to risk that again. Especially with a woman who'd done to another man exactly what Meg had done to him.

Well, hell, he told himself as his thoughts circled crazily, he hadn't gotten away from a damn thing. He'd dragged them all here to town with him. He forced thoughts of his family and the woman to the back of his mind and concentrated on the meeting.

Caleb sat in the back of the room, listening to everyone talking about the upcoming elections. Hell, he didn't have time to serve on the board, so he had to admire those who were willing to not only put in the time, but put *up* with the constant stream of complaints from the members.

The meeting was in the main dining room, mostly because it was big enough for everyone to be comfortable. And, you could get something to eat or drink if you felt like it. The TCC was a legend in Royal. The building itself had taken a beating over the years, but the club had been undergoing some renovations recently.

The dining room was big, with dozens of tables covered in white linen. There was a fireplace, empty now, since even a summer night in Texas was hotter than hell. The walls were dotted with framed photos of members through the years. There were historical documents— including a signed letter from Sam Houston himself and even the original plans for the club, drawn up more than a hundred years ago.

Tradition ruled the TCC and every member there had a long history with the place, through family or marriage. Caleb's father had been a member, and so were the Goodmans. Simon was at the meeting tonight, too, shooting glares at Caleb from across the room. He really had to fire that man.

"So, thinking about running for president?"

Laughing, Caleb slid a look at Nathan Battle sitting beside him. They both had a beer in front of them but they'd been nursing the drinks all night since they both had to drive home.

"Yeah," Caleb said, "right after I run naked down Main Street."

Nathan grinned, leaned back in his chair and shook his head. "Feel the same. Man, you couldn't pay me to be on the board and put up with all the politics and the fights."

Caleb shook his head and watched James Harris break up a heated argument that probably would have become a fight in a few more minutes. A rancher and horse breeder, James was tall, African American and gravitated toward calm, which served him well as president of the TCC. Caleb was pretty sure the man actually *enjoyed* being in charge of the club.

"Look at that, how he can calm folks down without breaking a sweat. I swear, if James wasn't glued to his ranch, I'd hire him as a deputy." Nathan sighed. "My new deputy could learn a few things."

"Well," Caleb said, "now that James has got his nephew to raise, I think he's stepped up his patience game."

True. James had been named guardian of his eighteen-month-old nephew and Caleb admired how he'd stepped up to the new challenge. Couldn't be easy, ranching and being a single father to a baby.

"Simon Goodman's giving you looks that could kill," Nathan pointed out.

"Yeah, I know," Caleb said. "I'm ignoring him."

"Good luck with that." Nathan leaned closer to whisper, "Tell Shelby I'll be going to see Simon tomorrow about getting her money back. I wanted to give him some time to cool off."

"Yeah, I don't think that's happening." Caleb told his friend about Jared's visit to the ranch the day before.

"Damn it, Caleb." Nathan took a swig of his beer and winced as if it tasted bad. "You realize you just made this worse by lying about you and Shelby…"

Caleb thought about yesterday with Shelby. And last night. And this morning. He scrubbed one hand across his face, but it didn't do much to wipe away the mental images that were burned into his brain. Shelby naked in his bed. Shelby crying his name as an orgasm rocked her. Shelby rising up over him as she took him into her body, bowing her back, her long, thick hair falling across pale, smooth skin.

"You *were* lying, right?"

"What?" He looked at his friend and saw suspicion on Nate's features. "Sure. Of course."

His eyebrows lifted.

"All right, I don't know," Caleb said. He took a sip of his own beer. "There's something there. I just don't know what it is."

"I hate complications," Nate muttered.

"You're telling me," Caleb agreed.

Then James called the meeting to order. "All right everybody," he said, "if you'll settle down, we've got a few things to discuss tonight, but first, Gus Slade wants the floor. He's come up with a fund-raising idea that I

think is interesting. I hope you all agree to take part—
I sure as hell am."

Gus stepped up and laid out his plans for a bachelor
auction to benefit pancreatic cancer research. And while
he talked, Caleb glanced around the room. A few of the
men his age looked intrigued by the idea, which Caleb
did *not* understand. Damned if he'd put himself on the
auction block for a night out on the town.

James's expression didn't give away what he was
thinking—but of course as president, he'd be in the
auction, too. Just another reason to not be on the board.
Daniel Clayton appeared to hate the idea, yet in the
next second, he was announcing that his grandmother
was insisting he take part and so should everyone else.

Caleb couldn't be persuaded to enter, but after a
back-and-forth discussion, it was decided to go ahead
with the auction. Gus looked happy about it, James
looked resigned and most of the younger members were
downright eager. Took all kinds, Caleb thought.

A few hours later, Shelby was wide-awake. Her bedroom was dark and outside the night was quiet and still.
She saw headlights spear through the blackness and
knew that Caleb had gotten home from his meeting.
She was tempted to go and find him, tell him to talk
to her. Find out what exactly was going on with him.

But the truth was, she didn't want to know. How
could he have gone from the world's greatest lover to a
distant, cool stranger in the blink of an eye? Was it possible that the fire between them had already burned out?

Or was he deliberately pouring water on it?

"You're being ridiculous," she told herself, her whisper lost in the empty room. There was no relationship

here. She'd only known the man for a *week*. But a voice in her head argued, *Yes, but what a week it's been.* True, they'd been through a lot in just a short amount of time. But the moment his family showed up, he tossed her aside. He couldn't have made himself any more clear.

She heard the click of the doorknob turning and her breath caught as her bedroom door swung slowly open. Shelby's heart gave a hard thump in her chest as Caleb walked into the room.

Moonlight drifted through the window, illuminating everything in a soft glow. He was wearing black slacks, a white shirt, open at the neck, and his hair looked as though he'd been shoving his fingers through it.

"Sorry," she said wryly. "I didn't hear you knock."

He walked to the foot of her bed and stared down at her. "Yeah. That's because I didn't."

He stared at her for a long minute—long enough for Shelby to shift position uneasily. It seemed he was finally ready to talk. Whether she wanted to or not.

"How was your meeting?" She didn't care about the meeting, but she couldn't stand the strained silence another moment.

"What?" He shook his head. "Oh, that. Fine. How was your night?"

"Aren't we polite?" she murmured and had the satisfaction of seeing one of his eyebrows wing up. "My night was fine. Quiet. I organized the pantry in your kitchen."

"The pantry?" He frowned.

"Where the food is?" The longer this went on, the more impatient Shelby became. "Did you really come in here to talk about nothing?"

"No," he said abruptly and shoved both hands into his pockets.

"Then why are you here, Caleb?" Shelby threw the duvet off and climbed off the bed. Foolish or not, she felt better, more sure of herself, standing on her own two feet. "You ignored me all day. Left tonight without a word and then walk into my bedroom unannounced. What's going on with you?"

The moonlight accentuated the grim slash of his mouth and the frown etching itself between his brows. Ridiculous that what Shelby most wanted to do was *soothe* him. She should want to kick him.

"It's you," he said abruptly. "Damn it, this is all about you, Shelby."

There went the softer instincts.

"No," she said, firmly shaking her head. "You don't get to blame this on me." She walked around the side of the bed to stand right in front of him. "You're the one who changed, Caleb. The minute your family showed up, you turned into the Iceman."

His scowl deepened and she wouldn't have thought that possible.

"So you just don't want them to know that we—"

"We what, exactly?" he interrupted. "Slept together? Nobody's business but ours."

"Then *what* is it?"

He looked down at her, staring into her eyes with such concentration, it felt as if he were looking all the way into her soul. "I can't get my mind off of you," he admitted finally.

"And that's a bad thing?" she asked.

"It is," he said flatly, and his eyes flashed with temper she knew was directed internally. "I don't want to want you, Shelby."

She huffed out a breath to disguise the hard lump that had settled in her throat. Honesty might be the best policy but it was a bitch to hear it.

"That's very flattering, thanks." She folded her arms across her chest in a defensive posture. After the night they'd spent together, to hear him dismiss her like that was more than hurtful. It was devastating. And it shouldn't have been.

She never should have let herself care. Let herself be pulled into a situation that she had *known* wouldn't last. But it had happened anyway. Shelby couldn't even pinpoint exactly when she had fallen for him. Maybe it had all started that first day, when she'd raced into his arms and he'd helped her when he hadn't had to. Maybe it was when he'd trusted her with his late mother's treasures. Or when he'd kissed her out on the range. Or when he stood between her and Jared even when she hadn't wanted him to be some shining knight in armor.

Whenever it had happened, Shelby now had to deal with the fallout. She'd come to Texas to marry a man she hadn't really loved. Now she was in love with a man who didn't want her. She was really batting a thousand in the romance department.

What she felt for Caleb dwarfed what she'd thought was love for Jared. Shelby hadn't wanted to admit even to herself that she was falling in love with Caleb, because that would only make it more real. But now, staring into icy-blue eyes, she knew it was true.

"I'm not trying to flatter you," he snapped. Pulling his hands from his pockets, he grabbed her shoulders and held on, pulling her close while still, somehow, keeping her at a distance. "I'm trying to be honest, here. There can't be anything between us, Shelby."

"Oh, you're making that clear," she said tightly and squirmed to get out of his grasp.

He held on more tightly. "I don't want to want you, but I have to have you."

She went absolutely still. His eyes were fire now, ice melted away in a passion she recognized and shared. It was so stupid, she told herself, even as her body hummed into life. Why should she sleep with him when he'd made it plain he didn't want to care? But how could she love him and *not*?

"You're making me crazy, Shelby," he ground out, his gaze moving over her, his hands sliding from her shoulders to cup her face in his palms. "Can't stop thinking about you."

She covered his hands with hers and took a deep breath. "Why do you want to?"

He bent his head, kissed her, then stared into her eyes again. "Because it's better for both of us."

"You're wrong," she said. "And I can prove it to you." Shelby went up on her toes, wrapped her arms around his neck and kissed him as she'd been wanting to all day. Her lips parted over his and her tongue swept in to claim his. He reacted instantly, jerking her close, holding her so tightly to him she could feel his heartbeat pounding against her. Breathing was fast and hard.

His mouth devoured hers and she took everything he offered and returned it to him. His hands snaked up under her tank top and cupped her breasts, his thumbs and fingers tweaking and tugging at her nipples until everything in her melted into a puddle of need. Her fingers stabbed through his hair, holding his head to hers, his mouth to hers.

Shelby's entire body was throbbing, her heart was racing and her blood felt thick and hot as it pumped through her veins. When he stripped her top off and bent his head to take one nipple then the other into his mouth, she swayed unsteadily and kept a tight grip on his shoulders to balance herself.

Caleb tipped her back onto the bed and she went willingly, eagerly. Shelby tore at his shirt, sending tiny white buttons skittering across the floor. She didn't care. She wanted to hold him, feel him.

"I missed you today," she admitted, kissing his shoulder, trailing her lips and tongue along his heated skin until she found the spot at the base of his throat that she knew drove him wild.

He groaned, tipped his head to one side and gave her free access. Shelby lavished attention on him, licking, nibbling until he stabbed his fingers through her hair and pulled her head back. "I missed you, too."

His mouth covered hers as she shoved his shirt off his shoulders and down his arms. Her fingers went to his belt and undid it, then unhooked the waistband of his slacks and slid the zipper down. She reached for him and sighed when her hand closed around the hard, solid length of him.

His hips rocked into her hand and he threw his head back and hissed in a breath. She half expected him to howl and everything in her fisted into tight knots of expectation. Anticipation. She stroked him, rubbed him, caressed the tip of him with the base of her thumb until he trembled and Shelby thought there was nothing so sexy as a strong man being vulnerable.

"Wait, wait," he ground out and pulled away from her.

"Come back," she said, coming up onto her knees to crook one finger at him.

He sighed. "Oh, yeah." Then he stripped, pausing only long enough to grab a condom from the pocket of his slacks. "Stopped at my room before I came here."

"I like a man who thinks ahead," she said and slowly shimmied out of her tank top. Moonlight pearled on her skin and she loved the flash in his eyes as he stared at her.

Then he was back on the bed with her and he was pulling her sleep shorts down and off, running his hands over her behind, stroking the hot, damp core of her. Shelby was writhing, twisting in his grasp and as the promise of another earth-shattering climax hovered closer, she reached for him. "Inside me, Caleb. Be inside me again. I need to feel you."

"What you do to me," he said, shaking his head as he watched her. "All I can think about is being with you. In you."

"Then *do it*," she demanded.

Nodding, he flipped her over onto her stomach and before Shelby could even manage a response, he was lifting her hips until she was kneeling. She looked over her shoulder at him and felt fresh need grab her by the throat. He looked dark, dangerous and deadly sexy. His skin was tanned, his body rock hard and as he smoothed on the condom, her heart leaped into a gallop.

Then he was behind her, sliding into her and Shelby cried out his name. He held her hips in his big, strong hands and rocked in and out of her in a fast, breath-stealing rhythm. She had no choice but to follow his lead. She curled her fingers into the sheet beneath her and held on.

She pushed back against him, moving with him, taking him higher and deeper than she would have thought possible. He became a part of her. Shelby didn't know where she ended and he began and she didn't care. All that mattered was what he was doing to her, making her feel. Her body erupted and she turned her face into the mattress to muffle the scream torn from her throat.

Shelby was still trembling, still shaken when Caleb shouted out her name and his body slammed into hers, giving her everything he was and promising nothing.

Nine

The Courtyard shops were a few miles west of downtown Royal. It used to be a ranch, but when the owners sold off, the property became an eclectic mix of shops. The latest was a bridal shop and Shelby had taken a moment to look through the window. In just ten seconds she'd seen five prettier gowns than the one she'd been forced to wear to her disastrous almost wedding.

A large, freshly painted red barn housed Priceless, the antiques shop, plus a crafts studio where people could come in and try their hands at everything from painting to ceramics and more.

Several other buildings on the property showcased local craftsmen such as artists, glassblowers and soap and candle makers. Local farmers rented booths to sell their fresh produce and canned goods and there was even a local cheese maker who always had a long line of customers.

Shelby loved it all. Actually she pretty much loved everything about Royal. Small town life really agreed with her. She wasn't looking forward to moving back to Chicago once she got her money from the Goodman family.

Which should be soon, since the sheriff had told Caleb that he was going out there today to take care of things.

And that left her exactly where?

Shelby sat at a small, round table outside the tiny coffee shop and sipped at a tall glass of iced tea. August hadn't cooled off any and she couldn't help but wonder what winter in Texas would be like.

But she didn't think she'd be finding out.

Watching people stroll past her, some hand in hand, Shelby sighed a little. Last night, she and Caleb had come to a détente of sorts. He didn't want to care for her and she couldn't care for him. It didn't matter how she felt because he wouldn't want to hear it.

"What a mess."

"Excuse me. You're Shelby Arthur, right?"

The woman was blonde, with big blue eyes and a wide smile. She wore a pale green summer dress that showed off tanned, toned arms and legs.

"Hi, yes."

"Do you mind if I sit down and talk to you for a second?" Without waiting for consent, she pulled out a chair and sighed as she sat. "I'm Alexis Slade and thanks for sharing the shade under your umbrella."

"No problem." Shelby smiled at her. "Didn't I just see you at Priceless?" She had been at the antiques store, to talk to Raina Patterson about the last load of crystal and glass they'd taken in. Raina already had buyers for most of the items and the others she would sell in her shop and pay Caleb when they sold.

She should have felt a lot of satisfaction for how Caleb's house was turning out with a little organization. Instead, she was sad because it seemed that her time in Royal was quickly coming to an end. But she shook off those feelings and concentrated on Alexis.

"Yes. I was there to talk to Raina about a fund-raiser the TCC is going to be putting on."

"Oh." Shelby nodded. "Sure, the bachelor auction. Everyone here is talking about it."

Alexis rolled her eyes, set her cream-colored bag on the table and dug out a notebook. When she flipped it open to an empty page she sent Shelby a wince of embarrassment. "I know. Paper and pen. I'm practically a cave person. But it's so much easier for me to just write things down."

"I do the same thing," Shelby assured her as a hot wind blew through the courtyard, tossing her hair across her eyes. She plucked it free, then asked, "But what did you want to talk to me about?"

"I'm not ashamed to admit that I need help," Alexis said, smiling. "You know, I run our family ranch, the Lone Wolf, with no problems at all. But running this auction and getting things like invitations and sponsors for prizes and the bachelors all lined up is giving me a headache."

"I can imagine." She tried to sound sympathetic, but Shelby couldn't help but feel a quick zip of excitement. There was nothing she liked better than taking over a confused mess and bringing order to it.

"Raina was telling me what a great job you did out at Caleb's ranch, organizing his mother's collection…"

"It's been challenging," she admitted, "but yes, it's all coming together."

"Well," Alexis said with another smile, "I figured if that didn't scare you off, then maybe I could find a way to coerce you into helping me get this auction off the ground?"

A little boy careened past the table, trailing a helium balloon in his wake. His giggles floated like soap bubbles on the air. A waitress came out with a fresh glass of tea for Shelby and one for Alexis, though it hadn't been ordered.

"Thanks, Ella," Alexis said on a sigh. "You're a lifesaver."

The young woman grinned. "You want your usual salad, too? Or something else?"

Alexis looked at the brownie on the table in front of Shelby and winced. "I'll have one of those, please, and screw the calories."

Shelby laughed and Ella said, "In this heat, you'll burn them right off as soon as you eat them."

Once they were alone again, Shelby said, "I'm happy to help, but I don't know how long I'll be in town."

Alexis sipped at her tea. "So you've decided to move back to Chicago when you get your money back from Jared?"

Shelby's jaw dropped and her eyes went wide. "Wow. Small town grapevines are really impressive."

"Yeah, sorry." She smiled and shrugged. "But I was at the wedding that didn't happen."

"Oh, God."

"Hey, don't worry about it," Alexis said and reached out to give Shelby's hand a reassuring pat. "I totally understand. I mean, I know you and Caleb are together and how could you marry Jared when you loved someone else?"

"Oh, Alexis, we're not—" God, she had to clear this up. People were talking and that wasn't fair to Caleb, even though he was the one who'd said it, feeding Margaret's gossip until it had become a huge blob of innuendo with a life all its own.

"I felt the same way, you know?" The friendly woman leaned back in her chair, crossed her legs and said, "Back in high school, Jared asked me out constantly, but I didn't go out with him because I was crazy about someone else..." Her words trailed off and a thoughtful frown etched itself briefly on her features.

She knew how Alexis had felt. Shelby was crazy about Caleb. And crazy for letting her emotions get so deeply involved. It was one thing to make a mistake unknowingly. But when you walked right into one with your eyes wide-open, that had to be nuts.

"Anyway," Alexis said and thanked Ella when her brownie arrived, "will you help me get this started? I'd be so grateful."

Shelby thought about it and realized that even if her time in Royal was short, she had to keep busy. Otherwise, she would torture herself with wishing things could be different with Caleb.

"I'd be happy to."

"Great!" Alexis pulled a pen out of her purse and looked at Shelby in expectation. "So. Where do we start?"

Shelby laughed and proceeded to do what she did best.

"Time we talked."

Caleb glanced over his shoulder and watched his

younger brother walk into the shadowy barn. "Not now."

"Yeah," Mitch countered, still walking toward him in a determined stride. "You've been saying that for four years now."

"Then I probably mean it." Caleb turned back to the stall door and stroked the nose of the mare poking her pretty head out for some attention. Just last night, she'd had her foal and done it all on her own, with no supervision from the local vet.

He had a million things to do and not one of them included talking to his brother about ancient history. Caleb took a deep breath, letting the familiar scents— straw, horses, leather and wood—soothe him. But that didn't last because it seemed his brother was determined to finally have his say.

"Damn it, Caleb," Mitch said, stopping right beside him. "What the hell did you expect Meg and me to do?"

"You don't want to do this, Mitch. Just let it lie."

"You mean let's just go on like we have been?" Mitch asked, throwing his hands high then letting them slap back down against his thighs. "With you acting like you've still got a knife in your back?"

Caleb shot him a hard look and turned away, headed for the wide double doors. Mitch stayed with him, finally reaching out and grabbing his brother's arm to stop him in his tracks.

"Nobody wanted to hurt you," Mitch said quietly.

"Didn't stop you, though, did it?"

Mitch yanked his hat off and rubbed his hand back and forth over his nearly shaved head. "No. It didn't. Nothing would have stopped me from having Meg."

Caleb winced. That's how he'd felt about having

Shelby. Instantly, images from the night before filled his mind and his body went tight and hard. The woman had touched something inside him that he hadn't even known was there. But as much as he wanted her, as much as being inside her burned him to a cinder, how could he trust her? How could he trust any woman enough again to risk the kind of humiliation he'd already lived through once?

Mitch drew his head back and stared at him. "You're not still in love with Meg, are you?"

"What?" Caleb exclaimed. "No."

Just the thought of it shocked him. He hadn't been bothered by Mitch and Meg being happy together on the ranch. Not jealous or even bitter about what they'd found together. It was the betrayal that had hit him harder than anything else. And wasn't that enlightening? If he'd really loved Meg in the first place, it would have driven him crazy watching his brother with her.

What did that say? Hell, looking back now, he wasn't even sure he'd loved her *then*. He'd wanted to be married. To have a family. And Meg was the one he'd chosen to fulfill the role of wife and mother. God, had he been that big an ass?

"That's good to know. I always admired you, Caleb. You know that. But Meg." Mitch shook his head and gave a wistful smile. "Hell, we'd all known each other for years and then that summer it was like I was seeing Meg for the first time. Love just slammed into us both. Neither of us was expecting it or looking for it. It was just *there*. And when you find something like that, you can't just turn from it."

He could see that now, with four years of clarity behind him. And, maybe, Shelby dropping into his life gave Caleb a little more insight into how it must have been for his brother. Still… "Running away the night before the wedding wasn't the way to handle it."

"Yeah, I know that. And you should know, Meg didn't want to do it. I talked her into making a run for it. Cowardly? Okay, yeah it was." Mitch nodded thoughtfully. "But damn it, Caleb, you were always so damn self-righteous. So sure of yourself and how the world ought to run. If we had come to you, would you have listened?"

He hated to admit it, but the answer was most likely *no*. He'd had his plan and he wouldn't have listened to anything that would disrupt that plan.

"Maybe not," he allowed.

Mitch blew out a breath. "Thanks for that. And you should know we're both damn sorry for what we put you through. Hell, Caleb. I'm sorry."

Caleb nodded and looked at his brother. It had been four years since they'd really had a conversation that didn't revolve around the ranch. And it felt *good* to get this out in the open. To hopefully get past it.

"You and Meg are good together," he said finally and watched his younger brother's smile broaden.

"I love her like crazy," Mitch said. "More even than when I married her."

"Yeah. I can see that." Caleb slapped one hand against Mitch's shoulder and took a step that would end the enmity between them. "I guess things worked out just how they should in the end."

"You mean that?"

"Yeah," Caleb said, a little surprised himself, "I do."

"Good. That's good." Mitch nodded and blew out a breath again. "You know, you're gonna be an uncle again."

"Is that right?" Caleb grinned at the thought and realized that the hurt of four years ago was well and truly gone now. He could enjoy his brother. And his sister-in-law. He could put the past where it belonged and reclaim his family.

So, a voice in his mind whispered, *does that mean you can put what Shelby did aside and take a leap of faith?*

He shook his head to dislodge that thought, because he just didn't have an answer for it. Caleb could understand what Meg and Mitch had done, but the bottom line was, Shelby was a different matter altogether. How could he trust her to stay when she'd run out on Jared? She hadn't done it for love. She'd simply bolted when she couldn't handle the thought of going through with the wedding. If he took a chance with her, would she run again when things didn't go her way?

Shaking his head, he pushed those thoughts aside for now. He had no answers anyway. So he looked at his brother and said, "Let's go up to the big house and have a beer. We should talk about the new ranch land we're buying and the oil leases are coming due again in six months. We need to decide if we want to renew or start drilling ourselves."

Mitch settled his hat on his head and grinned. "Sounds good to me."

As they walked, Caleb was glad to finally be more at ease with his brother. But thoughts of Shelby made sure he wasn't at ease with anything else.

Cam had left a big bowl of pasta salad in the fridge and roast beef sandwiches on a covered plate for their dinner. After a long hot day, it sounded perfect. But for right now, Shelby sat at the kitchen table, making a list of things for Alexis to look into for the auction.

First, of course, had to be advertising. If they really wanted to make the most of this auction, then they needed as many single women as possible to take part.

"Houston papers as well as Royal," she murmured, making notes as she talked. "A website would be good, too. Maybe they could have a link on Royal's town site, but one of its own would be even better."

"Talking to yourself?" Caleb asked as he came into the room.

She looked up and smiled. Memories flooded her mind, how he'd been last night, how *they'd* been, together. Maybe she should have been embarrassed but instead all she could think was that she wanted to do it all again. And again.

Squirming a little on the bench seat as her body warmed, she forced cheer into her voice. "No, I actually told Alexis Slade I'd help her with the bachelor auction."

Caleb went to the fridge for a bottle of beer. Once he had it open, he took a long drink and shook his head. "Can't believe they're going to do it."

"Are you going to be one of the bachelors?"

"Oh, that's a big hell no," Caleb said, firmly shaking his head for emphasis.

Foolishly, relief washed over Shelby. Heck, she might not even be in Royal when the auction happened, but she was glad to hear he wouldn't be bought by some woman who wasn't *her*.

"I think it sounds fun," she said, deliberately making herself smile. "We're thinking of a Christmas theme."

"Christmas? It's *August*," Caleb pointed out.

"Well, it's not going to be held tomorrow. The auction is set for November, so a Christmas theme will really work. There's a lot to be done in not very much time." She looked back to her list and started a new column for decorations. "Plenty of mistletoe, and wreaths and ribbon. Probably a hundred yards or so of ribbon, since Alexis says they're holding the auction at the TCC in the gazebo. To make it look like a winter wonderland it will take a few miles of pine garland and red ribbon—"

"Ribbon."

"And snow." She looked up at him. "Does it snow in Texas? Heck, does it ever cool off in Texas?"

He grinned. "It doesn't usually get cold enough to snow."

"Fake snow, then. It could be mounded in corners with little signs pointing the way to the dessert tables and the bar and the auction itself… Ooh, write that down. We should have lots of different desserts. I bet Jillian at Miss Mac's Pie Shack would do the desserts for us and—" She paused and narrowed her eyes on him. "What're you smiling at?"

He shook his head. "Just that I'm sort of getting used to your monologues."

"Well," she said, "I talk to myself because I always understand me."

"Uh-huh." He walked to the kitchen island, hitched one hip against it and asked, "How do you know Jillian Navarro at Miss Mac's Pie Shack?"

"I was in town and hello. *Pie.* I stopped in to try some and got to talking with her, and her daughter is just adorable and her desserts are amazing."

"Right. So you're helping Alexis with the auction. Making friends all over town. Does that mean you've decided to stay in Royal after you get your money back?"

Shelby sighed. She'd been thinking a lot about just that. Stay or go. The truth was, she had nothing in Chicago to go back to. A few friends, some loyal clients, but nothing else. Here in Royal, she could start over. Build a new business. Make new friends. But even she didn't believe those reasons were the only ones she was considering staying for.

She'd like a chance with Caleb. But there was no guarantee that would happen and if she stayed and couldn't have him, would she be able to live with it?

"Honestly, I don't know," she said, looking up at him. "Until I get the money, I don't have to make that decision so I guess I'm putting it off."

He simply stared at her for a long minute or two and once again, Shelby was left wishing she could read what he was thinking. The whole quiet cowboy thing was irritating in the extreme when you wanted answers and got nothing but more questions.

Then his manner shifted. He straightened up, set his beer down on the counter and pointed at the window behind her. "Looks like we've got company."

Shelby turned in her seat in time to see Brooke Goodman get out of her car. Darkness was lowering over the ranch, but the porch light was bright enough to see that Brooke's light blond hair was lifting in the ever-present wind. She wore skinny black jeans, a dark red shirt with long sleeves and a pair of black sandals. She took a long look at the house, then turned back to her flashy red convertible and reached into the backseat.

When she lifted out one of Shelby's suitcases, Shelby gave a *whoop* of excitement. "She's brought my stuff!"

Jared's sister was the only one of the Goodman family that Shelby had actually *liked*. Brooke had been her one and only bridesmaid at the wedding that hadn't happened. And if she was here now, with her suitcase, maybe she was also going to deliver the money that was Shelby's.

She scooted out of the bench seat and headed for the door. "I'll go talk to her."

"Yeah," Caleb said, walking right behind her. "*We* should."

Shelby rolled her eyes. Whether he wanted her or not, the man couldn't seem to stop trying to protect her. But with Brooke, no protection was necessary.

She opened the door just as Jared's sister was lifting one hand to knock. Instead, she slapped that hand to her chest and gave a short laugh.

"Wow. You scared me."

"Sorry," Shelby said and reached out to hug her. "I'm so glad to see you, Brooke."

"I'm sorry it took me so long to get your things back to you," she said, as Caleb took the suitcase from her and pulled it inside. "There's another one in the backseat."

"I'll get it."

Meanwhile, Shelby steered Brooke into the great room and took just a second for a little self-congratulatory smile. She really had made a huge difference in this house. The room was open, welcoming. The ranch was now looking exactly like what it was, a luxury ranch house with eclectic details. She waved Brooke onto the couch and sat down beside her.

Brooke was petite and pretty and so nice it made up for the fact that she seemed nearly perfect. She was also a talented artist, though neither of her parents were supportive of her goals.

"Thank you for bringing my things," Shelby said.

"Don't thank me." Brooke took a breath and let it out in a rush. "I couldn't get your money. The family is still furious and it was all I could do to sneak your suitcases out."

Shelby felt a wave of disappointment rise up, then dissipate. She would get her money, it was just a matter of *when*. "It's okay. Really." She forced a smile. "This is all my fault, anyway. I should have called the whole thing off long before the wedding day."

Brooke shook her head. "Don't ruin it for me. You're actually my hero in all of this. You stood up to the Goodman family and that's something I've never been able to do."

Shelby knew that Brooke's dream was to go to Europe to study painting, view the old masters in person. But her parents had control over Brooke's inheritance and they refused to give her what her grandmother had left her.

"Brooke," Shelby said, reaching out to give her hand a squeeze, "just *do* it. Don't wait for your parents to agree. Just go."

The other woman sighed a little. "I can't touch my money unless my parents give permission or I'm married."

"Wow." Shelby sat back. "Couldn't you go anyway? Work to support yourself while you're there?"

"It sounds wonderful, but I'm not trained to do anything," Brooke said. "Unless someone wants me to arrange a sit-down dinner for thirty. I can do that."

"You're being too hard on yourself," Shelby said.

"You're so talented. You have to do something with your art."

Brooke instantly brightened. "Actually, Alexis Slade asked me to do some painting at the TCC. I'm doing a mural at the day care and more in the public garden areas. It's not Europe, but it's exciting."

Shelby grinned. "What did your parents say?"

Brooke laughed. "They don't know."

Caleb walked back into the room and took a seat near the two women. "I put your things in your room, Shelby."

"Thanks. Brooke was just telling me—"

"What the hell?" Caleb cut her off, looking through the wide front windows at a long, black sedan hurtling down the drive and coming to a hard stop behind Brooke's car.

Both women turned to look and Brooke groaned. "Oh, God. That's my father. What's he doing here?"

"He probably knows you brought my things over," Shelby said, standing up. "I'm so sorry. You shouldn't have to get in trouble over me."

"Doesn't matter," Brooke said. She stood up, too, and all three of them watched as Simon Goodman stomped toward the front door.

He didn't bother to knock, just came inside and slammed the door behind him. "Brooke! Where the hell are you?"

She gave Shelby a sad smile. "Right here, Father."

Caleb took a step forward, automatically putting himself between Simon and the rest of the room. He stood there, Shelby told herself, like a soldier. Back straight, legs braced wide apart, arms crossed over his chest. He was a solid wall of protection and she felt a rush of warmth for him. He would always stand for someone he felt needed defending.

Simon Goodman marched into the room like a man on a mission. His features were thunderous, his dark eyes burning as he swept the room before landing on his daughter. "The minute I saw that woman's suitcases gone from the hall, I knew you were behind it."

"Father," Brooke said with calm, "these are Shelby's things. She deserves to have them."

"She deserves *nothing* from us," he countered and shifted his gaze to Shelby. "You've dragged my son's name through the dirt. And for what?"

Caleb speared him with a hot look. "You're going to want to watch what you say, Simon."

"It's all right, Caleb. I can handle this," she said, then looked at the older man vibrating with fury. "Mr. Goodman, I didn't mean to—"

"You didn't mean," Simon said with a harsh sneer. "Is that supposed to make this all go away? People are gossiping about my son and here you are, living with a rancher, no better than you should be."

Caleb took a step closer to him. "That's enough, Simon."

The older man glared at him. He wore a suit and tie, but his hair was disheveled as if he'd been electrocuted recently and his eyes fired with indignation.

"It's not enough. You were a guest at my son's wedding and left with the bride." Simon looked him up and down with one quick, dismissive glance. "What does that make you? Or *her*?"

"Now, just a minute," Shelby said.

"Father, you're making this worse."

"You keep your mouth shut," Simon snapped. "You're a damn traitor to your family."

"Hey, there's no need to punish Brooke," Shelby protested.

"Simon," Caleb warned, ice dripping from his words. "You should leave. Now. You don't need to be here."

"I'm here to deliver this tramp's money." He reached into his inner suit pocket and pulled out a check. Then he tossed it at her and watched as it fluttered to the floor.

"Pick it up." Caleb's voice was cold. Tight.

"Damned if I will," Simon said.

Brooke bent to pick up the check and instantly handed it to Shelby. "I'm sorry for all of this," she whispered.

"Sorry? You're sorry?" Her father's eyes wheeled. "This woman smeared your family, your *brother* and you would apologize to her?"

He looked back at Shelby, a sneer on his face. "There's your damn money." He shifted his gaze to Caleb. "I brought it because I had to see this tramp myself. To tell her that she should leave Royal because a life here will be a misery for her." He looked at her. "I'll see to it myself."

"You'll do *nothing*." Caleb moved in on the man and Shelby noticed how quickly Simon backpedaled.

Still, she didn't want to cause even more chaos in this house. This town. "Caleb, I told you I don't need to be defended."

"There is no defense for you, young woman," Simon blustered.

Caleb ignored him and focused on Shelby. "You think I don't know you can handle this? I do. But I'm damned if I'm going to stand in my own house and listen to insults."

"It doesn't matter," Shelby insisted. "Not to me. Not anymore."

Brooke put one hand on her arm and shook her head slightly, as if silently telling Shelby to let Caleb handle it.

"It matters to me," Caleb said. "I've seen more of the Goodmans in the last week than I have in the last year and I can truly well say that but for Brooke, I've had more than enough."

"You would insult me? Your father wouldn't stand for this," Simon said.

"Well then, that convinces me I'm doing the right thing." Caleb took another step closer to the other man. "You're fired."

"What?" He genuinely looked surprised.

"Should have done it years ago, but it's done now."

"Caleb," Shelby said.

"You're going to let this woman ruin a good working relationship?" Simon was clearly stunned at the idea. "Are you blind, boy? She's just a city girl come looking for a rich cowboy. She turned my boy loose and she's aiming at you, now."

"Oh, for…" Shelby muttered.

Caleb never glanced at her. "You should leave, Simon. Your business is done here."

"You'll regret this, boy."

"Not a boy," Caleb reminded him. "And the only thing I regret is waiting so long to fire your ass."

"Brooke," Simon ordered, "you go get in your car. We'll not stay and be insulted."

"Brooke," Shelby said quietly, "you don't have to go."

"Now," Simon roared.

"It's better if I go," Brooke said. "Don't worry. He's all thunder, no lightning. I'll talk to you soon."

Simon stomped from the room and Brooke was just a step or two behind him. She turned at the threshold and gave them one small smile before following her father out to the yard.

Caleb and Shelby stood side by side, watching as the Goodmans drove off. Shelby was more than a little rattled by the encounter, but her suitcases were in her room and she held a check in her hand. She glanced down at it, making sure the total was right. It was.

Caleb looked at it, too, then caught her gaze with his. "So, guess there's nothing holding you here now, right?"

She lifted her gaze to his and wanted to wail when she saw the blank look in those icy-blue eyes. Just a moment ago, he'd stood in front of her, defending her. Now it was as if he'd erected a wall between them, closing her off, turning her back into the outsider she had been when she'd first come here.

"I don't know," she said simply. "I don't know what I'm going to do."

"Come on, Shelby." He shook his head, his gaze locked with hers. "We both know what you're going to do."

"No—" She didn't. How could she know when everything inside her was in turmoil?

"You'll go back to Chicago, now that you've got the means to do it," he said in a clipped tone that carried a sheen of ice. "Your reason for staying's gone. Probably best all the way around. No point dragging this out, is there?"

God, it was as if he'd already said goodbye and

watched her leave the ranch. Was it so easy for him, then? To let her go? Would he not miss her? Even a little? "Caleb..."

He spoke up quickly as if he simply didn't want to hear whatever she might have said. "I don't blame you for leaving. Royal's not your home. Nothing holding you here anymore. Sorry you had to go through all of that, but at least it's finished now." He took a step back from her.

"I've got things to check on," he muttered. "Don't wait on me for dinner. Don't know when I'll be back."

Shelby watched him go and knew he was doing more than walking out of the room.

He was walking out of her life.

Ten

Two days later, Shelby was still in limbo, and it was a cold, lonely spot.

Caleb had cut her out of his life with the smooth efficiency of a surgeon. Yes, she was still living at the ranch, but she might as well have been on the moon. Caleb didn't come to her in the middle of the night. They didn't share dinner in a quiet kitchen, telling each other stories of the day. She hadn't been back in *his* room since their first night together.

In the mornings, he left at first light, so she didn't even see him over the coffeepot. And Shelby tried to avoid the kitchen altogether now, since the sympathy in Cam's eyes simply tore at her.

"If you had any sense, you'd just leave," she told herself firmly.

She'd taken her check and opened a bank account in

town. But that didn't necessarily mean she was going to stay, she reminded herself. She could always have the money wired to another account. In Chicago. Or maybe New York. Or even Florida. Somewhere far away from Texas so she didn't have to be reminded of what a nightmare the month of August had become.

"Sorry," Meg said as she hurried back into the twins' bedroom. "Sometimes I hate that phone."

"It's okay," Shelby said, putting on a smile and a lighthearted tone that she didn't feel. No reason to depress Meg. Especially since the woman was giving Shelby something to *do*. Something to focus on besides her own broken heart. "Gave me a chance to look around, get some ideas."

"Thank God," Meg said, doing a slow circle to take the room in.

Just like the main ranch house, Meg and Mitch's place quietly spoke of money. There was nothing overt, but the furnishings were all high quality and the house itself had obviously been built with care. Hardwood floors gleamed in slashes of sunlight that speared through wide windows. Heavy rugs dotted the floors, giving warmth to the space and the twins' beds were side by side, divided only by a child-sized table holding a grinning, cow-shaped lamp.

The space was huge and Shelby's imagination raced with ideas for making the space more like a child's dream room.

"You know, with the new baby coming, I really want to get Jack and Julie's room redone. And with the miracle you worked at the big house, who better to help me?" Meg walked over, picked up a pair of Julie's pink sneakers and stowed them neatly beneath the bed.

Shelby nodded thoughtfully as her mind whirled with idea after idea. "I love how it is right now. It's decorated beautifully."

"It is, but it's more adult pretty than kid pretty, you know?"

Shelby knew just what she meant. The furnishings were lovely, but there was nothing about the room that sparked a child's imagination.

Meg looked around again. "We had a designer come in originally, but—" she winced "—the woman didn't actually *have* children, so she set the room up as if kids never move or do anything. I mean, it's pretty and I do like it, but the toys and clothes and just the general flotsam created by two tiny humans is staggering. Even the housekeeper is ready to throw up her hands."

Shelby grinned. "Well, I don't have kids, either, but I know what I'd like. I think there are a few simple things we can do to make it all easier on you and them."

"I'm all ears," Meg assured her.

"Organization first, and then we can spruce it all up and make it more…fanciful."

"I like it already," Meg assured her.

Shelby walked to the wide walk-in closet and threw the doors open. "This for example. There's a lot of wasted space. On hangers, kids' clothes don't hang down very low. We can put a shelving system here and add wicker baskets on the bottom. That way the kids can put their own toys away in the baskets while you'll have the top shelf for shoes, sweaters, whatever else you need, but don't hang."

"I like it," Meg said, nodding as if she could see it.

"And, we can have beds made that come with storage beneath, so the twins can have their own treasure chests, keep things that are important to them stored away."

"Oh, they'd love that," Meg agreed.

Shelby gave an inner sigh. Those children were adorable and pulled on every one of her heartstrings. Along with giving her own biological clock a good, hard kick.

She shook the feeling off and concentrated on bringing her imagination to life. "And in the corner, we can put in a table and chairs, kid-sized, where Julie can practice her drawing. With a series of smaller shelves and small baskets there, we'd have a space for her paper and crayons and markers."

Meg grinned. "Oh, my God, this is great. Keep going!"

Laughing now, Shelby turned and pointed to the far corner. "This room is so big, we could build a playhouse there for both of the kids and make it like a tree house." She was thinking as she spoke and smiled when another idea hit her. "You know, Brooke Goodman is an excellent artist. I bet she'd love to paint a tree mural on the wall and we could build the house to look as though it's hung on the tree branches. With little steps and ladders and secret passages… Oh, and maybe a place inside where they could nap."

"I love it. I love all of it," Meg said, wrapping her arms around her middle. "I can't even tell you. It's perfect. Honestly, Shelby, you're brilliant."

"Thank you, but sometimes, it just takes an outsider to look at a space and see it differently."

Meg frowned a little. "You're not an outsider, Shelby."

Shaking her head, she ignored that because the truth was that Caleb had cut her out. Pushed her out.

"I just love to bring a room together and make it functional, you know?" She looked around and could almost see what it would be like when it was finished. A sharp pang settled around Shelby's heart when she realized she most likely wouldn't see the completed project. How could she stay when Caleb was making it clear he didn't want her there?

"This is more than functional," Meg said. "You're talking about building a kid's dream room."

Shelby smiled. "For now. Then, when they want their own rooms, you could make this one a shared play space and decorate other bedrooms for them."

"God knows the house is big enough for it," Meg said, nodding. "And Mitch is already talking about adding on another wing. The Mackenzies are big on *wings*," she added with a laugh. "He wants a *lot* of kids, but then, so do I."

"It sounds wonderful," Shelby said and, though she thought she was being stiff-upper-lippy, Meg must have caught something in her tone.

"What's going on, Shelby?"

"Nothing. Really." Even she heard the lie and Shelby wished she were better at it.

"Is it you and Caleb?"

Shelby shook her head. There really was no point in pretending, when she'd have to leave the ranch soon. Everyone would know the truth then. "There is no me and Caleb."

"What? Why? Since when?" Meg walked closer. "I can see the way you look at each other. Your eyes practically devour him when he walks into a room. And he's clearly crazy about you, Shelby."

"No, he's not," Shelby said and looked down into the

yard. From the kids' bedroom, she had a good view of the corral where Caleb was working with one of the horses. He held the reins as the huge, black animal trotted around the perimeter. Mitch and the three-year-old twins stood at the fence, watching, but Shelby couldn't tear her eyes away from Caleb.

Everything about that man called to her. Sadly, he obviously didn't feel the same about her. Otherwise, he never would have been able to simply ignore her existence as he had the last couple of days.

"What happened, Shelby?" Meg asked, her voice soft. "Did you guys have a fight?"

Shelby laughed, but it hurt her throat. "No, we didn't. That's the hardest part to accept. Nothing happened. Nothing at all. No fight. No huge, defining moment that tore us apart. It might be easier to take if there had been a big blowup." She sighed a little and kept her gaze locked on Caleb. "He just...shut down. Shut me out. The Goodmans gave me my money and Caleb assumed I'd be going back to Chicago. He actually told me it was probably for the best."

"Idiot," Meg muttered.

Shelby smiled sadly at the camaraderie. "After that, he simply closed himself off. For the last two days, he's ignored me completely. Avoided me. He won't even talk to me, Meg. I don't even know why I'm still here."

She turned to look at the other woman. "At this point, I think maybe Caleb was right and it would be for the best if I just left. For both our sakes."

"Oh, God, I was afraid of this." Meg sighed and moved up to stand beside her at the window. "This isn't about you, Shelby. This is about me."

Confused, she turned to look at her friend. "What do you mean?"

"God, it's like a Karmic circle."

"What are you talking about?" Shelby asked. Misery was stamped on Meg's features but her eyes simmered with a low burn.

"This is about me. And Mitch and what happened four years ago." Meg turned around to look at Shelby. "Once upon a time, I was engaged to Caleb."

Stunned, Shelby stared at her. She hadn't known what to expect, but this was still a shocker. Caleb was always so cool with Meg, it was hard to imagine the two of them engaged. "Really?"

"I know. Weird to think about now. It's funny, but Caleb never even really proposed." Meg sighed, reached up and tucked her hair behind her ears. "It seemed like a natural progression, you know? We'd known each other forever. He wanted family and so did I and..." She sighed. "That sounds so lame, but—"

"It's okay," Shelby assured her. Hadn't she done the same thing with Jared? Given in to her need for family, for home and then come to regret the decision? "Believe me, I understand."

Meg gave her a weak smile. "Thanks. Anyway, long story short—a few weeks before the wedding, Mitch and I discovered we loved each other. But what could we do? I was engaged to his brother for heaven's sake. Neither of us wanted to hurt Caleb, but that's what we did."

This explained so much, Shelby thought. Why Caleb would pull back every time a connection began to grow between them. And knowing this, she didn't have a clue how to fight it. How to get through to him and expect him to trust her.

"At the time, I tried to find a way to talk to Caleb, but he's so damn single-minded he wouldn't listen." She held up one hand. "Don't misunderstand, I'm not saying that any of this was his fault. Mitch and I were in love and it seemed like there was only one way to be together. So, the night before the wedding, Mitch and I eloped."

"Oh, God." Shelby shifted her gaze to the man in the middle of the corral.

"Yeah." Meg stood beside her. "I left Caleb a letter, trying to explain it all, but of course it wasn't enough. Apologies weren't enough. And for the last four years, Mitch and I have tried to make it up to him, but that's hard to do when the man won't acknowledge your presence."

"I know that, too," Shelby murmured.

"Caleb and Mitch kept working together, but they used to be close and that ended when we eloped. I still feel guilty about that. I know that it hurts Mitch daily. And I think Caleb misses his brother, too." Meg took a breath and sighed it out. "Just the other day, though, Caleb and Mitch talked and it might be getting better between them. But he'll never forgive me."

She turned, and her gaze locked with Shelby's. "So when you ran out on your wedding, it really hit home with him."

"Of course it did." Shelby's heart actually *sank*. She felt it drop to the pit of her stomach where it sat like an icy stone. This was why she couldn't get past the wall he'd built around himself. This was at the heart of the darkness she'd glimpsed in his eyes a few times.

No wonder he couldn't trust her. She understood how it had to seem to him. Shelby had done to Jared exactly

what Meg had done to him. He'd already experienced
betrayal and didn't want to risk it again.

"I'm so sorry, Shelby. He's being an ass because of
something I did."

She wanted to agree. A part of Shelby wanted to give
Caleb that out. Let him off the hook. But by doing that,
she heaped guilt on Meg's head and she wasn't willing to do that.

"You know what?" Shelby said with a slow shake
of her head. "No. It's not your fault. You did the right
thing four years ago just like I did the right thing. Caleb
should know that."

"Yes, but—"

"No. If he doesn't want to trust me, then he has to
do it for real reasons. For things I've done—well, okay
I did run out on my wedding, so yeah. But I didn't do
it to Caleb. Why should he expect that I'd be untrustworthy? I'm practically a golden retriever I'm so loyal."

"A dog?"

"And he should know that," Shelby said, getting an-
grier the longer she thought about it. "We've been together nonstop for nearly two weeks. And in dating
time, that's like two years or something—"

"Well, two years is—"

"He should know me better," Shelby continued, talking to herself more than Meg. She stared out the window at Caleb's broad back and half expected him to
turn around and look at her just from the power of her
stare. "And if he doesn't know me better than this, then
he should have *told* me what he was thinking. Heck,
he's still mad at you and Mitch for not talking to him.

"Told me himself that I should have talked to Jared,
but *he* doesn't have to talk. No, not the great Caleb

Mackenzie. He gets to keep his secrets," Shelby muttered, warming now to her rant and letting it all out as she stared down at the man she loved. The man she was suddenly furious with.

"He just walks out and then ignores me. Does he tell me why? *No.* Did he hope I'd just go away? Slink out of town to make his life easier? Well, why would I do that? He should have talked to me, damn it. He's acting like a child and I don't like it one bit."

"Shelby—"

"Why should I go back to Chicago?"

"Who said you should?" Meg was watching her warily.

"Caleb tried, but why does he get a say in what I do when he won't even talk to me? No, I don't want to go back. I was going to anyway, because it was too hard to be here and not be with Caleb. But that would make it easy on him, wouldn't it? And why should I do him any favors? Why does he get it easy when *he's* the reason this is all happening?"

"Um," Meg said, "I don't know."

"If Caleb Mackenzie wants to ignore me, then I'm going to make him work for it." Shelby turned around and headed for the door, riding a wave of anger. "I'm staying in Texas. I'm staying in Royal. And I'm going to start up my business and I'm going to be so successful he'll hear my name everywhere he goes."

"That's great, but—"

Shelby stopped at the threshold and looked back at her friend. "The good news is, I'll be here to help you make this room fabulous. And I'm going to help Lucy Curran, too. And help Alexis run the auction. And we'll design your new baby's room together, too, and when you're ready to add on the new wing, we can plan it all out together."

"Yay?" Meg said, clearly a little shocked at how quickly Shelby had moved from misery, to sympathy to fury. "Um, where are you going now?"

"To tell that stoic cowboy that he loves me. And to let him know that if he can't trust me, then it's his loss." She didn't wait to see if Meg had a response.

Shelby took the wide staircase at a fast clip, crossed the elegantly appointed hall and went out the front door. She walked straight to the corral and paused only when the kids rushed up to her.

"Sheby!" Jack looked up and shouted, "I get a puppy!"

Shelby's heart melted a little at the way Jack mutilated her name.

Julie was there, too. "*We* get a puppy! He's mine, too."

"Is not."

"Is, too."

Mitch came over, scooped up both kids into his arms and grinned at Shelby before telling his kids, "It's my puppy! Let's go find Mom so we can go get that poor dog that's going to be killed with love."

"Yay!" The twins shouted in excitement as their father carried them off to the house. Then she turned back to Caleb, still in the corral, busily ignoring her.

Now that she knew what was behind his behavior in the last few days, she was torn. She loved him. And she was furious with him. She wanted to kiss him and kick him. Shelby wondered if most women felt that way.

"Caleb!"

He glanced over his shoulder at her. "I'm busy."

"That's too bad," she said and kept walking. She was wearing her pale green camp shirt, white capris and completely inappropriate sandals to be walking through the dirt, but that couldn't be helped. She wasn't going to stop now.

Opening the corral gate, she started inside when Caleb shouted, "Stay outside! I don't want you near this horse, he's still a little wild."

Well, that stopped her cold. She was angry and ready for a come-to-Jesus meeting, but she didn't want to be killed by a horse, either. "Fine. Then you come out. We have to talk."

He glared at her for a long minute and she wondered how she could be both angry and attracted at the same time. The look on his face was fierce and it didn't bother her a bit. If anything, it made her insides churn with the kind of longing that had been eating at her for the last few days.

She watched as he released the lead from the horse's bridle, then turned him loose to race crazily around the corral. Caleb walked to the gate and opened it, closing it again securely behind him. Then he didn't glance at her before heading for the barn.

Shelby was just a step or two behind him. "Will you stop so we can talk?"

"Whatever we have to say to each other is going to be private," he growled out, "not said out in the yard where every cowhand nearby can listen in."

"Oh. All right."

In the shadowy barn, Caleb finally stopped, turned around to look at her and said, "What is it?"

Huh. Now that she had his complete attention, she hardly knew where to start. But that irritated gleam in his eyes prompted her to just jump in, feetfirst. "Meg told me what happened four years ago."

"I'm not talking about that," he said and turned away.

She grabbed his arm and he stopped. "Fine. We don't have to. But we do have to talk about the fact that it's the reason you're shutting me out."

"Don't be ridiculous."

"I'm not. You don't trust me, Caleb." It broke her heart to say it, to read the truth of it in his eyes as he looked down at her. "Because I did to Jared what Meg did to you. So you're thinking that I'm completely untrustworthy. But I'm not. I did the right thing in walking away. It wasn't easy, but I did it."

"I didn't say I don't trust you."

"Oh, please, you didn't have to," she countered, waving him into silence. Horses in their stalls moved restlessly. The scent of straw and wood and leather surrounded them and she knew it was a scent she would always associate with Caleb.

"I understand why you feel that way, but you're wrong."

"Well, thanks. Now I'm going back to work."

"I'll just follow you until I say what I have to say," she warned.

He believed her and sighed irritably as he crossed his arms over his chest. "Fine. Talk."

"You love me, Caleb."

He blinked at her. "What?"

"You love me and you don't want to and that's sad for both of us because we're really good together. I mean, I know we've only known each other a little while but like I told Meg, we've been together nearly every second, so that's like two years' worth of dates and really, does it matter how long you know a person before you love them?"

She answered her own question. "It really doesn't. The love is either there or it's not and it is. For you. And for me. And you don't want to admit it because you're scared."

"Scared?" He laughed, dismissing the very idea.

But Shelby knew him well enough to see the truth in his eyes. "Terrified. You know, I was going to leave Royal. Because I knew you didn't want me here anymore so I thought it would be best if I just left. Make it easier on you—"

He opened his mouth to speak but she cut him off.

"—but I don't want to make it easy on you. You *should* suffer because I'm here in town but not with you. Because it'll be your own fault because you're too stubborn to see that what Meg did four years ago was right. And what I did was right, too. Doing the right thing isn't always easy, Caleb. But it's necessary. I still believe that. And did you ever think that maybe fate brought me here to Texas so that I could realize a mistake and find *you*?"

"Fate?"

She kept going. "Just so you know, I'm opening my business in Royal and I'm going to work for Lucy Curran. And Alexis. And I've got a job working with Meg, too, so I'll be here at the ranch. A lot. So get used to seeing me. And not having me."

Her heart was breaking, but she also felt good, telling him exactly what she was thinking, feeling. How could she have fallen for a man so stubborn? So resistant to the very idea of taking a chance again?

"You should know that I love you, but I'm going to

try to get over it." She turned around and headed for the door, determined to get out before she cried. After that wonderful speech, she didn't want to ruin it all by looking pitiful. Which is just how she felt, beneath the simmering boil of anger.

"Where the hell are you going?" Caleb shouted.

"To Royal," she called back. "I'm going to buy a house."

An hour later, Caleb was still thinking about what she'd said. And how she'd looked, facing him down, challenging him, calling him a damn coward.

Was she right?

She was staying in Royal. She'd be right there. In town. Every day. And she wouldn't be with *him*. Is that what he really wanted? Caleb had spent the last two days ignoring her, avoiding her, because he thought it best to get used to being without her. So it wouldn't hit him so damn hard when she left for Chicago.

But she wasn't leaving.

And he missed her already, damn it.

"Uncle Caleb!" Julie's voice and the clatter of tiny feet stomping into the barn.

"Look! A puppy!"

Grateful for the distraction from his own thoughts, Caleb looked up to see the twins rush inside, a black Lab puppy in Jack's arms. A local rancher's dog had had another litter and Mitch had been determined to get one of the pups for the twins. Looks like that, at least, had gone well.

Meg was right behind the kids, though, so his smile didn't last long.

"He's a girl," Jack said proudly.

"She don't have a name," Julie announced.

"Doesn't," Meg corrected. "You kids set the puppy down, but keep an eye on her while I talk to your uncle, okay?"

As the kids settled in to play with the puppy who was busy peeing on the straw floor, Caleb drew a sharp breath and narrowed his eyes on her. Setting things right with Mitch had been one thing. But he didn't know that he was ready to talk to Meg about any of this. Hell, he'd had too much already of strong-willed women. "I'm busy, Meg."

"You're always busy, Caleb. But this little chat is long past due." Meg reached out and stroked the long nose of a mare who'd stuck her head through the stall door hoping for attention. "I told Shelby she could use my car, so she's in Royal right now, looking for a place to buy. Or rent."

"She told me."

"Uh-huh, and you're still standing here, so I'm guessing you didn't listen to anything she said any more than you've ever listened to me." She gave him a look he'd seen her pin the twins with and he didn't much care for it.

Then he glanced at the kids shrieking and laughing with their pup. "Now's not the time for this."

"Now's the perfect time," Meg corrected. "I knew you wouldn't be rude to me in front of the twins."

"So you used them."

"You bet," she agreed. Laying one hand on his forearm, Meg leaned into him and said, "You're a good man, Caleb. But you're being deliberately deaf and blind."

"Butt out, Meg," he warned quietly.

"No, I've done that for too long." Smiling sadly, she

said, "We were friends once, Caleb. Good friends who made the mistake of thinking that meant a marriage would be good for us, too.

"We were wrong. I'm sorry I hurt you when I ran out on the wedding, but can't you see now that I did the right thing? For all of us? You and I are too much alike, Caleb. We're both so damn quiet usually that we never would have spoken to each other."

He thought about that for a second and had to agree. Mitch was the louder brother and he kept Meg laughing. Just as Shelby did for Caleb. Already, he wasn't looking forward to the silence that would greet him in the house every day once Shelby left for good. Hell, the last two days had been bad enough, even knowing she was there.

"Damn it, Caleb, everyone can see that you feel for Shelby what I feel for Mitch." Meg looked up at him, serious and determined. "You and I would have made each other miserable. But you're happy with Shelby. The two of you just *work*."

He sighed, looked over her head at the slash of sunlight outside the barn. In his mind's eye, he could see Shelby in those foolish sandals, marching through the dirt and straw, her chin held high, riding the mad she had for him. He saw her in Houston, wearing that blue dress, laughing up at him.

And he saw her in bed, hair a wild tumble, her eyes shining and a soft smile on the lips he couldn't taste enough.

"Don't hold what I did to you against Shelby, Caleb," Meg was saying. "Don't cheat yourself out of something spectacular because you're holding on to old hurts. Oh, and by the way, I'm glad you and Mitch worked things out. He's missed you, you big jerk. I've missed you."

He blinked at her and laughed. She was standing up for Mitch as he stood up for Shelby and Caleb realized that she was right. Had been all along. Yeah, he wished they had handled it better, but Mitch and Meg were good together. As he and Shelby were.

For the first time in four years, he could look at his sister-in-law and not be reminded of betrayal. Which told him that he was the only one who had been preventing his family from healing. Maybe Shelby had a point. He'd never thought of himself as a coward, but what else could you call a man who refused to forgive? Refused to trust? Refused to grab his future because of his past?

He'd hated the thought of Shelby moving away from Royal, going back to Chicago or wherever. But he hated even more the idea that she would be living in town without him. He couldn't stand the thought of being without her damn it and she was right. He did love her. He just hadn't wanted to admit it, even to himself.

Idiot.

"I hate lectures, Meg. You know that."

"Yes, but—"

"Especially," Caleb added, "when you're right."

"I am?" A slow, self-satisfied smile curved her mouth.

"Don't gloat," he said, giving her a one-armed hug that eased away the last of the pain, the last of the aloofness he'd treated her with for too long.

When she hugged him back, Caleb relaxed. "Hell, I have been blind. I see how good you and Mitch are together, Meg. And I'm glad of it."

She tipped her head back and smiled, her eyes shining. "Don't cry."

"Absolutely not," she said, shaking her head as a single tear dripped down her cheek. "Pregnant hormones. I'm good. So what're you going to do now?"

Only one thing he could do. "I'm going to Royal and I'm going to bring Shelby back home. Where she belongs."

Shelby liked the condos well enough, she thought as she walked down Main Street. But after living at Caleb's ranch, they all felt small, confined. There was no view of ranch land or ancient oaks. There were no kids playing in the yard and mostly? There was no Caleb.

"You're going to have to get used to that, though," she muttered. She walked past Miss Mac's Pie Shack and waved to Jillian through the glass.

Across the street, she saw Lucy Curran and waved to her, as the woman hurried to her truck. Alexis Slade was heading into the TCC and Shelby realized that Royal had become home to her. She had friends here. Work here. She would be fine. She'd get over Caleb. Eventually.

"Shouldn't take more than ten or twenty years," she told herself.

Stepping up her pace, she hurried along to the TCC. If nothing else, she could go inside and tell Alexis that she was going to be staying in Royal, so she'd be available to help with the bachelor auction. "Keep busy, Shelby. That's the key. Just keep busy."

She heard the roar of the engine before she looked up to see it. Caleb's huge black truck came hurtling down Main Street and careened into the TCC parking lot.

Shelby's heart was pounding hard in her chest even before Caleb shut off the engine and leaped out of the truck, slamming the door behind him. Her mouth went dry and her stomach started spinning. He stalked toward her and his features were tight and grim.

"Caleb, what're you doing here?"

He moved in close, grabbed her upper arms and lifted her up onto her toes, pulling her face within a kiss of his. "Damn it, Shelby, what the hell do you mean you love me but you'll get over it?"

Surprised, she could only stare up at him as he loomed over her. The brim of his hat shadowed his face, but his eyes, those icy-blue eyes, were on fire. "Just what I said. I'm not going to be in love all by myself, how stupid would that be? So I'll just work on getting over you and—"

"Stop," he ground out. "Just stop and let me talk for once. There's a lot to say. A lot I should have said before now." He eased his grip on her arms, but he didn't let her go. "First things first, though. You're not in love alone. I love you, Shelby."

Her breath caught and she felt tears sting her eyes.

"You sneaked up on me," he said, his gaze moving over her face as if etching her features into his mind. "Before I knew it, I was loving you and trying not to."

"Great," she murmured.

He grinned, then sobered. "You're right you know, the time we've spent together is as good as two years of dating. I know you, Shelby," he said, his fingers gentling his hold on her but not letting go. "I know I can trust you. I know that. I was just…"

"A big stoic cowboy?" she finished for him.

"Yeah, I guess," he admitted wryly. His hands slid

up her arms to cup her face as his voice deepened and the fire in his eyes became a low, simmering burn. "The point is, I didn't want another woman in my life. I was so mad at Meg and Mitch and never took the time to notice that she was right to do what she did. Just like you were."

"Oh, Caleb…" He couldn't have said anything that would have touched her more.

"Not finished," he warned and gave her that half smile that never failed to tug at her heart. "I don't want you to ever get over loving me, Shelby. I need you too badly."

"I didn't want to get over you," she said softly, as she sensed that all of her dreams were coming true. "I love you, Caleb. I always will."

"I'm counting on that darlin'." He gave her another half smile. "I was an idiot. I didn't want to risk love again. Thought it was just too dangerous to even try. Since you, though, I realized that losing you would be the real risk— to my heart and my sanity. How the hell could I live in a quiet house? I'd miss those rants of yours."

"I'm going to choose to be flattered," she said, smiling up at him because her heart was racing and her hopes and dreams were about to come true, right there on the busy Main Street of Royal, Texas.

"Good. That's how I meant it." Caleb shifted one hand to cup her face and he said, "I love you, Shelby. Don't think I'll ever get tired of saying it. I know I'm not easy to live with—I tend to go all quiet and pensive—but I think you're tough enough to pull it off."

"I really am," she promised. "When you get too quiet, I'll just follow you around, or ride a horse out to find you and I'll stick to you until you talk to me again."

"You won't have to follow me, Shelby," he said, his gaze locked with hers. "We're going to be side by side. And we're going to have a hell of a good marriage and we'll make a lot of babies, fill up all those empty rooms with laughter and love. Because that's what you deserve. It's what we *both* deserve."

"It sounds perfect," Shelby said. "And I think we might have already started on those babies. Skipping a few days of pills probably wasn't a good idea."

His eyes went wide and bright and his smile was one that lit up every corner of her heart. "Yeah? That's great, because you know Meg's pregnant again, so they're three ahead of us."

"We'll catch up," Shelby said.

"Damn straight we will." Caleb leaned down and kissed her, hard and long. When he lifted his head, he said, "Let's go."

"Where?" she asked, a laugh tickling her throat.

"Down to the jewelers," Caleb said firmly. "We're picking out a ring. Biggest one he's got, because I want everyone who sees it to know you're mine and I'm yours."

"You don't talk a lot," Shelby said with a sigh, "but when you do, you say just the right thing."

"There's just one more thing I have to say," Caleb whispered.

"What's that?" What more was there? He'd already given her the dream. Home. Roots. Family. *Love.*

"Shelby Arthur," he said softly, "will you marry me tomorrow?"

She sighed, filled with the love she'd always longed

for and looked up into icy-blue eyes that would never look cold again. Then she grinned and asked, "Why not tonight?"

Caleb picked her up, swung her around, then planted another kiss on her mouth. "That's my girl."

* * * * *

LET'S TALK
Romance

For exclusive extracts, competitions
and special offers, find us online:

f facebook.com/millsandboon

⊙ @millsandboonuk

🐦 @millsandboon

Or get in touch on 0844 844 1351*

For all the latest titles coming soon,
visit millsandboon.co.uk/nextmonth